The story of PETER PAN has been inspiring children and adults
alike for over 100 years. Great Ormond Street Hospital
has been closely linked with PETER PAN ever since its author,
J.M. Barrie, generously gifted the rights to his immortal
classic to the hospital in 1929. A long-time supporter,
Barrie loved children and his exceptional gift was a natural
expression of that support. In his own words, during
a speech in 1930, 'At one time, Peter Pan was an invalid
in the Hospital for Sick Children, and it was he who
put me up to the little thing I did for the Hospital.'

As 2010 marks the 150th anniversary of Barrie's birth,
this limited edition has been published as part of
The Peter Pan Collection in aid of Great Ormond Street
Hospital Children's Charity, in partnership with Harrods.

Harrods is proud to celebrate this magical story of the boy
who would not grow up, a story that continues to help many more
children at Great Ormond Street Hospital to grow up today.

'I like well to be in the company of explorers'

J.M.Barrie

GERALDINE McCAUGHREAN

Peter Pan in Scarlet

Illustrated by DAVID WYATT

With the support of
Great Ormond Street Hospital Children's Charity

OXFORD
UNIVERSITY PRESS

OXFORD

UNIVERSITY PRESS

Great Clarendon Street, Oxford OX2 6DP

Oxford University Press is a department of the University of Oxford.
It furthers the University's objective of excellence in research, scholarship,
and education by publishing worldwide in

Oxford New York

Auckland Cape Town Dar es Salaam Hong Kong Karachi
Kuala Lumpur Madrid Melbourne Mexico City Nairobi
New Delhi Shanghai Taipei Toronto

With offices in

Argentina Austria Brazil Chile Czech Republic France Greece
Guatemala Hungary Italy Japan Poland Portugal Singapore
South Korea Switzerland Thailand Turkey Ukraine Vietnam

Oxford is a registered trade mark of Oxford University Press
in the UK and in certain other countries

Published with the support of Great Ormond Street Hospital Children's Charity

First published 2006
First published in this exclusive Harrods edition 2010

Acknowledgement is made to the Precentor and Director
of Music at Eton College for permission to use the
words of the Eton Boating Song.
'Dedicatory Ode' from *Complete Verse* by Hilaire Belloc (copyright ©
The Estate of Hilaire Belloc 1970) is reproduced by permission of PFD
(www.pfd.co.uk) on behalf of The Estate of Hilaire Belloc.

British Library Cataloguing in Publication Data

Data available

ISBN: 978-0-19-279268-6

1 3 5 7 9 10 8 6 4 2

Printed in Great Britain by CPI Mackays, Chatham ME5 8TD

Paper used in the production of this book is a natural,
recyclable product made from wood grown in sustainable forests.
The manufacturing process conforms to the environmental
regulations of the country of origin.

For all daring explorers,
and for Mr Barrie, of course

HOW THIS BOOK CAME ABOUT

First it was a play. Then it was a book. During the early years of the twentieth century, the story of Peter Pan was a runaway success which made James Matthew Barrie the most successful author in Britain.

In 1929, Barrie made a remarkable gift to his favourite charity. He gave away all his rights in Peter Pan to Great Ormond Street Hospital for Sick Children. This meant that whenever anyone staged a production of the play or bought a copy of *Peter Pan and Wendy*, the hospital would be the richer for it, instead of Barrie. Over the years, it has proved a more valuable gift than he could ever have imagined.

In 2004, Great Ormond Street Hospital decided to sanction, for the very first time, a sequel to the book *Peter Pan and Wendy*. They held a competition to find, from among authors all over the world, someone to continue Peter's adventures in Neverland. With a plot outline and a sample chapter, Geraldine McCaughrean won that competition. *Peter Pan in Scarlet* is the book she wrote. Now you can read it.

From quiet homes and first beginning,
Out to the undiscovered ends,
There's nothing worth the wear of winning,
But laughter and the love of friends.

Hilaire Belloc

CHAPTER ONE
The Old Boys

'I'm not going to bed,' said John—which startled his wife. Children are never ready for bed, but grown-ups like John are usually hankering for their pillows and eiderdowns from the moment they finish dinner. 'I'm not going to bed!' said John again, and so ferociously that his wife knew he was very frightened indeed.

'You have been dreaming again, haven't you?' she said tenderly. 'Such a trial.'

John scrubbed at his eyes with his knuckles. 'I told you. I never dream! What does a man have to do to be believed in his own house?'

His wife stroked his shiny head and went to turn down the bedclothes. And there on John's side of the bed, something bulged up through the coverlet. It wasn't a hot-water bottle or a teddy bear or a library book. Mrs John folded down the sheets. It was a cutlass.

With a sigh, she hung it on the hook behind the bedroom door, alongside the quiver of arrows and John's dressing gown. Both she and her husband liked to pretend it was not happening (because that's what grown-ups do when they are in trouble) but secretly they both knew: John was dreaming of Neverland again. After every dream, something was left behind in his bed next morning, like the stones around a dish after a serving of prunes. A sword here, a candle there, a bow, a medicine bottle, a top hat . . . The night after he dreamt of mermaids, a fishy smell hung about the stairs all day. The wardrobe was piled high with the dregs of dreams—an alarm clock, an Indian head-dress, an eye-patch, a pirate's tricorn hat. (The worst nights were when John dreamed of Captain Hook.)

Mrs John plumped up the pillows with a brisk blow of her hand—and a gunshot rang out through the whole house, waking the neighbours and terrifying the dog. The bullet shied about the room, bouncing off the lamp-stand and smashing a vase. Cautiously, with two fingers, Mrs John drew the pistol from under the pillow and dropped it into the bin, like a kipper found to be not quite fresh.

'They are so *real*!' whimpered her husband from the doorway. 'These wretched dreams are just so *REAL*!'

All over London and even as far afield as Fotheringdene and Grimswater, old boys were dreaming the same kind of dreams. Not young, silly boys but boys grown-up: cheerful, stolid boys who worked in banks or drove trains or grew strawberries or wrote plays or stood for Parliament. Cosy at home, surrounded by family and friends, they thought themselves comfortable and safe . . . until the dreams began. Now each night they dreamed of Neverland and woke to find leftovers in their beds—daggers or coils of rope, a pile of leaves or a hook.

And what did they have in common, these dreamers? Just one thing. They had all once been Boys in Neverland.

'I have called you all together, because something must be done!' said Judge Tootles, twirling his big moustache. 'It is not good enough! Gone on far too long! Won't do! Enough is enough! We must act!'

They were eating brown soup in the library of the Gentlemen's Club off Piccadilly—a brown room with brown portraits of gentlemen wearing brown suits. Smoke from the fireplace hung in the air like a brown fog. On the dining table lay an assortment of weapons, the sole of a shoe, a cap, a pair of giant bird's eggs.

The Honourable Slightly fingered them thoughtfully: 'The flotsam of Night washed up on the shores of Morning!' he said (but then the Honourable Slightly played the clarinet in a nightclub and was inclined to write poetry).

'Call Mrs Wendy! Mrs Wendy would know what to do!' said Judge Tootles. But of course Wendy had not been invited, because ladies are not allowed in the Gentlemen's Club.

'I say we should let sleeping dogs lie,' said Mr Nibs, but nobody thanked him, because dogs are not allowed in the Gentlemen's Club either.

'Mind over matter!' exclaimed Mr John. 'We must just *try harder* not to dream!'

'We tried that,' said the Twins mournfully. 'Stayed awake all night for a week.'

'And what happened?' asked Mr John, intrigued.

'We fell asleep on the London omnibus on the way to work, and dreamed all the way to Putney. When we got off, we were both wearing warpaint.'

'How perfectly charming,' said the Honourable Slightly.

'Last night we dreamed of the Lagoon,' added the second Twin.

There was a murmur of heartfelt sighs. Each of the Old

Boys had dreamed lately of the Lagoon and woken with wet hair, and dazzle in his eyes.

'Is there a cure, Curly?' enquired Mr Nibs, but Doctor Curly knew of no cure for an outbreak of unwanted dreams.

'We should write a letter of complaint!' boomed Judge Tootles. But nobody knew of a Ministry for Dreams or whether there was a Minister of State for Nightmares.

In the end, with nothing solved and no plan of campaign, the Old Boys sank into silence and fell asleep in their armchairs, their brown coffee cups dropping brown drips on to the brown carpet. And they all dreamed the same dream.

They dreamed they were playing tag with the mermaids, while the reflections of rainbows twisted around and between them like water snakes. Then, from somewhere deeper down and darker, came a hugely slithering shape that brushed the soles of their feet with its knobbly, scaly hide . . .

When they woke, the Old Boys' clothes were sopping wet, and there on its back, in the middle of the Gentlemen's Library was a prodigious crocodile, lashing its tail and snapping its jaws in an effort to turn over and make supper of them.

The Gentlemen's Club emptied in the record time of forty-three seconds, and next day Members everywhere received a letter from the management.

The Gentlemen's Club
Brown Street
off Piccadilly
London W1

23 April 1926

We regret to inform you that the Club will be closed for redecoration from 23rd April until approximately 1999.

Your obedient servants

The Management

In the end, of course, it *was* Mrs Wendy who explained it. 'Dreams are leaking out of Neverland,' she said. 'Something must be wrong. If we want the dreams to stop, we must find out what.'

Mrs Wendy was a grown woman, and as sensible as can be. She had a tidy mind. For six days in any week she strongly disapproved of dreams littering up the house. But on the seventh, she was not *quite* so sure. Recently she had begun hurrying to bed, eager for that twilight flicker that comes between waking and sleep. From behind closed eyelids she would watch for a dream to come floating towards her—just as once she had watched at her bedroom window, hoping against hope for a small figure to come swooping through the local stars. Each bedtime her heart beat faster at the thought of glimpsing the Lagoon again, or hearing the cry of the Neverbird. Above all, she longed to see Peter again: the friend she had left behind in Neverland all those years before.

Now Neverland was rubbing against the Here and Now, wearing holes in the fabric in between. Tendrils of dream were starting to poke through. All was not well. Somehow Mrs Wendy knew it.

'Perhaps the dreams are messages,' said one Twin.

'Perhaps they are warnings,' said the other.

'Perhaps they are symptoms,' said Dr Curly, putting his stethoscope to his own forehead and listening for the dreams inside.

'I'm awfully afraid they may be,' said Wendy. 'Something is wrong in Neverland, gentlemen . . . and that is why we must go back.'

CHAPTER TWO

First Find Your Fairy

'*Go back!?*'

Go back to Neverland? Go back to the mysterious island, with its mermaids, pirates, and redskins? The Old Boys snorted and blustered and shook their heads till their cheeks flapped. Go back to Neverland? Never!

'Preposterous!'

'Ridiculous!'

'Poppycock!'

'Fol-de-riddle!'

'I'm a busy man!'

In the rosy gloom of her parlour, Mrs Wendy poured more tea and passed round the cucumber sandwiches. 'As I see it, there are three problems,' she said, ignoring their cries of protest. 'First, we have all grown too big. No one but a child can fly to Neverland.'

'Exactly!' Judge Tootles looked down at the straining buttons of his waistcoat. Over the years, he had indeed grown too big, in every direction.

'Secondly, we can no longer fly as we could then,' said Mrs Wendy.

'Well, there you are, then!' Mr John remembered the evening when a boy dressed in a suit of leaves had flown into his life and taught him, too, to fly. He remembered leaping from the open bedroom window and that first heart-stopping moment when night had caught him in its open palm. He remembered dipping and soaring through the black sky, blipped by bats, nipped by the frost, keeping tight hold of his umbrella . . . Oh, how brave he had been in those days! Mr John gave a start as Mrs Wendy dropped a sugar lump into his cup with a pair of silver tongs: his thoughts had been up among the moonbeams.

'And before we can fly,' Mrs Wendy was saying, 'we need fairy dust.'

'Then it is plainly impossible.' The Honourable Slightly looked down at the breadcrumbs on his trousers, and a lump filled his throat. He remembered fairy dust. He remembered it glittering on his skin like water drops. He remembered the tingling sensation it sent racing through his veins. Even after all these years, he still remembered.

'I think it is best if we do not tell anyone we are going,' said Mrs Wendy. 'It might upset those we love. Also it might attract the attention of the newspapers.'

There did not seem to be any arguing with her, so the Old Boys wrote down what she said, in their appointment diaries, under the heading Jobs to be done:

- Must not be grown up.
- Must remember how to fly.
- Must find fairy dust.
- Must think of something to tell the wife.

'I think Sunday week would be best,' said Mrs Wendy. 'There is a full moon that night, and the children will not need collecting from school. With luck, this annoying cold of mine will have cleared up, too. So, gentlemen. Shall we say June the sixth? I am sure I can rely on you to arrange everything?'

The Old Boys wrote in their appointment diaries:

Sunday 6th June.
Go to Neverland

Then they sucked their pencils and waited for Mrs Wendy to tell them what to do next. Wendy would know. Why, even with a cold she did not need an appointment diary to remind her what jobs needed doing!

Next day, Mrs Wendy's cold kept her from going out, but the Old Boys found themselves in Kensington Gardens with butterfly nets, wandering up and down. Looking for fairies.

There was a stiff breeze blowing. Something white and fluffy brushed Mr Nibs's face and he gave a shriek. 'There's one! It kissed me!' And all the gentlemen went pounding after it. The wind was rising. Other scraps of whiteness scudded past, until the air seemed to be full of flying snowflakes all twirling and dancing, feathery light. The Old Boys trampled the grass flat with running to and fro, swiping at fairies, accidentally swatting each other, whooping and shrieking, 'Got one!'

'So have—OW!'

'Here's one, look!'

But when they peered into their butterfly nets, all they found were the fluffy seed-heads off summer's first dandelions. There was not a single fairy in among the dande-down.

All day they searched. As the sun went down and starlings gathered over the glimmering city, the Lost Boys hid themselves among the bushes of Kensington Gardens. Early stars ventured into the sky, their reflections spangling the Serpentine. And suddenly the air was a-flicker with wings!

Jubilant, the ambushers leapt out of hiding and ran to and fro, nets flailing.

'Got one!'

'By Jove!'

'Don't hurt them!'

'Ouch! Watch what you are doing, sir!'

'I say! This is ripping fun!'

But when they turned the nets inside out, what did they find? Midges and moths and mayflies.

'I have one in here! Definitely! Incontrovertibly!' cried Mr John, cramming his bowler hat back on to his head to trap the captive inside. The others gathered round, jostling to see. The hat came off again, with a sigh of suction; Mr John reached in with finger and thumb, plucked something out of the satin lining and held it up to show them—the iridescent purple, the shiny, flexing, turquoise body . . .

Only a dragonfly.

Mr John opened his fingertips, and eight pairs of disappointed eyes followed the lovely creature as it staggered and waltzed back towards the water.

'I don't believe there is a single fairy . . .' began Dr Curly, but the others felled him to the ground and clapped their hands over his mouth.

'*Don't say it! Don't ever say that!*' cried Mr Nibs, horrified. 'Don't you remember? Every time someone says they don't believe in fairies, a fairy somewhere dies!'

'I didn't say I didn't believe in them!' said the doctor, tugging the rumples out of his suit. 'I was only going to say, I don't believe there is one single fairy *here*. *Tonight*. *In this park*. I have mud on my trousers, insect bites on my ankles, and I have not eaten supper yet. Can we give up now?'

The other Old Boys looked around them at the twilit park, the distant, glimmering streetlamps. They looked at the soles of their shoes, in case they had trodden on any fairies by mistake. They looked into the water of the Serpentine, in case any of the stars reflected there were really fairies, swimming. No fairies, no fairy dust. Perhaps, after all, they would not be going back to Neverland.

'All for the best. Absurd idea,' growled Mr John, but no one answered.

The Honourable Slightly took from his pocket a gleaming bubble filmy with every colour of the rainbow.

'Last night I dreamed I was playing water polo with the mermaids,' he said. 'This was on my pillow when I woke.'

The bubble popped and was gone.

The park gates were locked when they got there. The Old Boys had to climb over, and Judge Tootles tore his best tweed jacket.

In the end, it was Mrs Wendy who managed it, of course. She led the way to Kensington Gardens next day, wearing a linen coat and a splendid hat with a feather in it.

'But we looked here yesterday!' her brother protested. 'There wasn't a fairy to be found!'

'We are not looking for fairies,' said Mrs Wendy. 'We are looking for prams!'

Twenty years before, the park would have been busy with nursery maids pushing pramfuls of babies up and down, filling them up with good fresh air. These days, nursery maids were a rarer breed. There were only three today, pushing prams, feeding ducks, wiping noses, picking up rattles thrown out on to the grass. It was a sight that always disturbed the Old Boys . . .

Once, Curly and Tootles, Nibs, Slightly, and the Twins had all been babies like those in the prams. Once, they had been tucked up, cosy and snug, boggling up at the sky with sky-blue, newborn eyes. But they had fallen out of their prams.

Got lost. Gone astray.

They had been handed in to the Lost-and-Found office, and stored under 'B' for babies, right between A for aquaria and C for cricket bats. No one had claimed them, and after a week or so they had been posted off to Neverland. There they had joined all the other Lost Boys, making do without manners or mothers, making do on make-believe meals and catching doses of adventure along with their captain, Peter Pan.

As a pram rolled past, Mr Nibs could not stop himself saying, 'Oh, do *please* take care of that baby, young woman! I know there's nothing so *very* terrible about being a Lost Boy, but even so, *do* take care that it does not fall out! Lost Boys are not all as lucky as we were! They are not all adopted by Mr and Mrs Darling and loved and cherished and blessed with custard tarts on Sundays and a university education!'

'Well, I never did!' exclaimed the nursery maid. 'I hope you are not suggesting I might *lose* a baby of mine, sir? As if I would! As if I'd ever . . .' But before she could work herself into a paddy, the baby in the pram started to cry.

Mrs Wendy had been leaning over the pram, using the feather from her hat to tickle the baby.

'What are you doing, madam?' said the nursery maid.

'That one can't abide feathers!'

'Oh drat,' said Mrs Wendy, vexed with herself and secretly with the baby, too. 'Mr Slightly, don't just stand there! Sing!'

And the Honourable Slightly (who, if you remember, played the clarinet in a nightclub), suddenly realized that the success of the whole plan depended on him. Scooping up the baby, he began to sing.

'*Orpheus with his lute, with his lute made trees . . .*'

It was no good. The baby howled more loudly still.

'*Oh, the grand old Duke of York, he had ten thousand men . . .*'

Still the baby wailed.

'*Come into the garden, Maud,*
For the black bat night has flown!'

'Now see what you done!' said the nursery maid, wincing at the noise and looking around for a policeman.

Mr Slightly went down on one knee: '*Mammy! Mammy! I'd walk a million miles for one of your smiles, my Ma-a-a-mmy!*'

And suddenly the baby laughed!

It was a noise like water gurgling out of a jug. It was so delicious that the nursery maid clapped her hands and giggled too. 'His very first laugh, bless him!'

In one movement, the Old Boys lifted their hats. Even Mrs Wendy unpinned hers. Then, to the nursery maid's astonishment, they tossed the baby back into its pram and went racing out across Kensington Gardens, jumping and reaching and wildly waving their bowlers and brown derbies.

'Well!' said the nursery maid. 'What is the world coming to!'

Among banks of orange aubretia, beside the war memorial, they caught him—a tiny, bluish mite, with red hair and eyes the colour of honey—a fairy! Like a robin out of an egg, he had hatched out of that baby's first laugh, you see, as all fairies do.

The Old Boys were tired and short of breath, but they were triumphant.

Mistakenly, Mrs Wendy called the fairy Con Brio, not knowing he came ready-fitted with a name.

'I am Fireflyer!' said the fairy indignantly. *'And I'm hungry!'*

So they took him to the Serpentine Tea Rooms and fed him on ice cream, scone crumbs, and cool tea before bearing him home aloft in Mr John's bowler, like a little eastern potentate. By the time they reached the house in Cadogan Square, the hat was slightly scorched, but it was also half full of fairy dust.

CHAPTER THREE
A Change of Clothes

'Do you know Tinker Bell?' asked Mr John.

I know everything, said Fireflyer. *What's Tinker Bell?*

Wendy had made a kind of tepee out of a lampshade for the fairy to live in, and now he was busy collecting provisions, in case of a bad winter.

'It is only June,' Mr Nibs pointed out.

I get VERY hungry, snapped Fireflyer. They had noticed this already, since Fireflyer had already plucked all the buttons off the Chesterfield sofa, the rubbers off three pencils, the tassel off the bell-pull, and Mr Slightly's bow tie. He was like a small squirrel, leaping around the room, sniffing and licking, and scavenging for food. *'What's Tinker Bell? Answer me!'* Fireflyer repeated. *'Fairies die if you ignore them.'*

The Twins explained how, years before, they had lived in Neverland, with Peter Pan and his trusty helper Tinker Bell the Fairy. They described how brave Tinker Bell had been, and how spiteful, how mischievous and how jealous, how beautiful and how . . .

'Not as beautiful as me!' Fireflyer interrupted. *'No one's as beautiful as me . . . or as hungry!'* and he nibbled a candle right through to the wick so that it fell over.

'I do not very well see how you could know Tinker Bell, you little rogue,' said Slightly, 'since you were born only yesterday. Ow!'

Fireflyer bit him in the thumb. *'I'm very backward, that's how! I know all kind of things that have done happening. I'm backward as a bee sting, me!'*

Slightly sucked his bitten thumb. 'And I say that, for a very small person, you tell extraordinarily big lies.'

The redheaded fairy beamed with delight, and bowed very low with an elegant twirl of both hands. From that moment on, he was devoted to Slightly, simply because Slightly had admired the size of his lies.

Despite all Mrs Wendy's warnings not to attempt flying until they were small again, the Old Boys could not resist trying. Judge Tootles actually grabbed Fireflyer and rubbed himself all over with the fairy, as with a bar of soap. Then he spread his arms and flew like a bird!

. . . Like a large ostrich, in fact. Or one of those shaggy rhea birds who peck you in the neck at the zoo. Tootles lumbered along for a furlong, flapping his arms, then ran out of breath, as flightless as a dodo.

Dr Curly, who was whippety-thin and very fit, did manage to fly to the top of a lamp-post, but lost his nerve and had to be rescued with a loft ladder. Mrs Wendy assured them, as she put the ladder away, that it would be all right on the night, but they were none too sure.

They watched the days go by like trains. Then suddenly the sixth of June arrived, and it was time to climb aboard it and set off for Neverland. Fireflyer had told them how it could be done. A change of clothes was called for.

All over London and as far afield as Fotheringdene and Grimswater, Old Boys got down old suitcases from their attics and took out all the courage they owned. They went to their banks and withdrew all the daring they had saved up over the years. They checked in all the pockets of all their suits and felt down the back of the sofa to muster all the bravery they could.

And still it did not seem quite enough.

They bought flowers for their wives, toys for their

children, and washed the windows for their neighbours. They applied for leave from work. They wrote letters to their nearest and dearest but tore them up again, because GOODBYE is much the hardest word to spell.

Bath-time came at First Twin's house and while his twin sons were splashing, he slyly picked up some of their clothes from the bathroom floor and stole out into the night.

Time for prayers came in the house next door, and Second Twin told his identical twin sons, 'Hands together; eyes closed,'—then pinched a school uniform and sneaked away on tiptoe.

At the Doctor's house in Fotheringdene, Curly reached out to steal his child's rugby kit . . . but the new puppy beat him to it, grabbing the collar and hanging on grimly. The animal growled and whined, and its claws scraped loudly on the polished floor. The child roused up—'*Who's there?*'—so there was nothing Curly could do but pick up both shirt and puppy and run.

Storytime came in Mr John's house, and Mr John read his little ones to sleep, took one last look, then crept to the door holding a stolen sailor suit. On the landing, he gave a guilty start, for there stood Mrs John. She knew, of course. Mr John had not breathed a word about the Journey, but she knew anyway. Wives do. Now she presented him with a packed lunch, a clean pair of socks, and a toothbrush. She

even ironed the sailor suit before he put it on.
'Take care, my love,' she said, kissed him fondly, and led
him to the front door. 'Do give my warmest regards to
Peter Pan.'

Judge Tootles realized, rather late in the day, that he
only had daughters. The thought quite unmanned him. His
fingers strayed to his large moustache and he stroked it
like some dear pet that he must leave behind because of
moving house.

Nibs . . . well, Mr Nibs simply could not do it. Standing
beside the bunks in the back bedroom, watching the
sleeping faces of his little ones, he simply could not imagine
going anywhere without them—ever. He resigned then and
there from the trip to Neverland. In fact he even woke the
little ones up to ask, 'What has Neverland got that could
possibly be better than you?'

And the Honourable Slightly Darling? Well, he sat alone
now in his elegant flat, nursing his clarinet. When Fireflyer
had told them the secret of growing young again, Slightly
had nodded but said nothing. He had watched the day
come nearer, and dreamed dreams of Neverland, but said
nothing. He had seen the others steeling themselves for the
adventure, dusting Fireflyer's lampshade each day for fairy
magic, getting ready to go . . . and still said nothing. Now he
sat in his elegant flat, his clarinet silent in his lap.

He was not one to spoil another chap's fun. That was

why he had not spoken up. And they had all forgotten—his adopted brothers and sister—that Slightly was a widower and had no children—no one whose clothes he could borrow, no one to make him young again.

Because, of course, that's how it is done. Everyone knows that when you put on dressing-up clothes, you become someone else. So it follows that if you put on the clothes of your own children, you become their age again.

In wardrobes and broom cupboards, hopping down lamp-lit streets, squeezing their heads through little neck-holes and their feet into tiny football boots; straining seams and tripping over dressing gown cords, dropping wallets and fountain pens, and pocketing puppies, the Old Boys struggled into their children's clothes. You may ask how it was possible for Judge Tootles to fit into a smocked party dress and ballet shoes. All I can say is that there was a tambourine moon shining, magic at work, and somehow all the hooks did up and all the buttons fastened.

Their minds filled up with thoughts of Neverland and of running away. Oddly, as they ran, their feet no longer avoided puddles but preferred to splash through them. Their fingers chose to blip metal railings, their lips to whistle, their eyes to shine.

Dr Curly felt good sense trickle out of his head like sand, to be replaced with squibs and sparklers. The Twins suddenly remembered each other's favourite fairy stories. Judge Tootles found she could see without her spectacles and, when she swung from the climbing frame in the park, her teeth did not throb. But her top lip felt oddly bare, since for everso long she (or rather he) had worn a great curling moustache there and she missed it now as you might miss a pet hamster.

As the Old Boys rubbed fairy dust into the napes of their necks, short, prickly haircuts grew silky beneath their fingers—except for Tootles, of course, who found she had long yellow plaits and knew ballet positions One to Five.

. . . But the Honourable Slightly had no children. So he sat in his elegant flat, feeling every one of his thirty years weigh on his shoulders. Tugging off his evening tie, he went early to bed, hoping at least to *dream* of Neverland.

As for Mrs Wendy, well, she wrote a letter to the household, explaining how she was going to visit a distant friend and would return very soon. Before she put on her daughter Jane's clothes, she darned the girl's slips, rubbed out her day's mistakes with an India rubber, crocheted a happy dream to slide under her pillow, and put her prayers in alphabetical order. Then she packed a few useful things in a wicker basket and wriggled into a small, clean sundress appliquéd with sunflowers and two rabbits.

'It is always so sultry hot in Neverland,' she told her sleeping child. '. . . How extraordinary! A perfect fit.' Surprised by the last sneeze of her cold, she quickly reached for a handkerchief from the pocket of her discarded gown, tucked it up her little puffed sleeve, then crept out on to the balcony.

As she combed her share of fairy dust through her hair, lists and birthdays emptied out of her head, along with politics and typewriting; poems and recipes. Even her husband became a shadowy recollection. Not her daughter Jane, of course. No mother could ever forget her daughter. Not under any circumstances. Not for a minute.

In the sky over Kensington Gardens, a flock of flying children gathered, like birds in autumn getting ready to migrate. They floated on their backs, paddled along on their fronts, rode on the warm updraught from the High Street chimneys and got grubby in the smoke. A strand of old fog unravelling over the River Thames made them cough.

Owls blinked in astonishment. Nelson on top of his column raised his telescope to his one good eye. Statues of famous men pointed and jumped from foot to foot. (One on horseback even bolted.) Policemen on their beats heard squeals of laughter, but looked in vain for someone to arrest.

'Where is Nibs?' called Wendy.

'Not coming!' answered Fireflyer.

'Where is Slightly?' John wanted to know.

'Not coming!' cried Fireflyer, glowing with glee.

'*Oh, yes I am!'* And Slightly came porpoising through the air, his wavy hair a-glitter with fairy dust. He was wearing an evening shirt whose tails came down past his nine-year-old knees and whose sleeves flapped way beyond his fingers. In his hand he clutched a clarinet, like a dueller's sword. 'I went down to the foot of the bed, you see! Haven't done it for twenty years! Right down to the end and beyond! I remembered, you see! You can end up *anywhere* if you dare to go right down to the bottom! Which way now, Fireflyer?'

'How should I know?' snapped the fairy.

But everyone else answered for him: '*Second to the right and straight on till morning!'*

At set of moon, after they had gone, the rain came down in exclamation marks.

The further they flew, the more they forgot of being grown-up and the better they remembered their days in

A Change of Clothes

Neverland. Sunshine! Leapfrog! Picnics! Into their heads tumbled daydreams and excitements. And all their feelings fizzed inside them, and all their muscles were twangy. They almost forgot to remember why they were making the journey.

'If the Redskins are on the warpath, I'm going too!'

'Do you think Tinker Bell will be pleased to see us?'

'Oh, will she be there, then, this Tinker Bell?'

'I can't wait to see Peter's face when I give him his presents!'

'I can't wait to see the mermaids!'

'I said, will Tinker Bell be there? Fairies die if you ignore them, you know.'

'I hope there are new villains to fight!'

'Do you think there will be *new* Lost Boys, as well?'

At the thought of that, there was a sudden silence. Of course it was altogether possible! Boys fall out of their prams all the time, and nursery maids are notoriously bad at noticing. In all likelihood Peter Pan had gathered a new band of followers around him since the days of Nibs, Curly, the Twins, Slightly, and Tootles.

'Will the underground den be big enough for us all to fit?' Curly wondered anxiously.

'Will the others even let us in?' whispered the Twins.

'They better had, or I'll beat down the door!'

'There might even be Lost Girls,' said Wendy, uneasily. 'Girls are so much sillier than they were when I was a baby.'

She was not at all sure she wanted there to be Lost Girls; without the right upbringing, girls can be so very . . . *domestic*.

Fireflyer the fairy, scorching between them like a hot cinder, suggested gleefully, *'Maybe Peter Pan will cull you if there are too many! That's what Peters do, isn't it?'* and the younger boys turned pale with fright.

'There is always the Wendy House,' Wendy told them soothingly. 'If the den is too crowded, we shall live there.'

'Yes, and no one can stop us!' declared Tootles. 'We built that Wendy House our own selves, for Wendy! And you can't keep a Wendy out of her own Wendy House!'

A flock of clouds bleated its way across the High Way, causing a traffic jam. Fireflyer darted in among them, stinging and biting until the clouds broke into a trot. And as the flock scattered, there beneath lay . . .

NEVERLAND!

A circle without a perimeter, a square without corners, an island without bounds: Neverland. Imagination had pushed it up from the bottom of the sea and into the daylight. Now bad dreams had summoned them back to it: the place where children never grow up!

Little did they know (or care) that back in their various homes, on dressing tables and bathroom sills, their abandoned wristwatches stopped at that exact same moment. For when a child is in Neverland, time should stand still.

A Change of Clothes

Their hearts rose into their mouths. There was nowhere like this! In all the round world there is nowhere like Neverland! And there it lay, spread out below them, totally and completely and utterly and absolutely . . .

changed.

CHAPTER FOUR

The One-and-Only Child

Despite flying into the brightness of morning, Wendy, in her flimsy sundress, gave a shiver, for the sunlight was thinner and paler than she remembered. The shadows were longer—some rocky pinnacles and pine trees had three or four shadows all sprawling in different directions. Wendy knew they had been right to come: all was not well in Neverland.

As they flew over the Neverwood, an ocean of golden, orange, and scarlet trees tossed and rolled beneath them now, loosing, from time to time, a spray of crisp, autumn leaves. The Redskin totem poles leaned at crazy angles, felled by wind or war, and roped in creepers and ivy. Huge globes of mistletoe rolled about the treetops like Chinese lanterns. It was beautiful . . . but there was no birdsong.

The clearings, where once the League of Lost Boys had built camp fires or held councils of war, were gone: healed up and disappeared as surely as a hole in the sea. If there were wolves lurking, they could not be seen. If there were Redskins on the warpath, their warpaths were hidden from sight.

'How shall we ever find the den or the Wendy House?' said John, voicing everyone's fears. But they need not have worried, for the little house with its red walls and mossy green roof was the very next thing they saw. The smoke from its chimney coiled between them and they reefed themselves in by it, hand over hand.

Wendy's House stood balanced on the branch of a tree—a tree taller by the height of a church spire than any in the forest.

'How amusing,' said Slightly. 'We had a tree in our house, before. Now the house is in the tree!'

'How can a tree be inside a house?' snorted John.

'Oh, but there was! Don't you remember? Down in the underground den? The Nevertree! Every morning we sawed it off at the floor, and by dinner time it had grown just the right height to use for a table.'

On the washing-line that stretched between two branches, wispy clouds hung snagged, alongside a wind-ragged apron, a flag, and a single sock.

'That is my apron!' exclaimed Wendy.

The flying children rapped at the door; they rattled at the windows and clamoured round the chimney pot. But no one came to let them in. After a night's flying, they were starting to tire.

'He has shut us out!' cried Wendy. 'After all he said! Me, I've never closed my bedroom window, winter or summer! Not ever since Neverland!'

'Not even in a fog?' asked Curly.

Wendy was forced to admit it: 'Well, perhaps in a fog. You know how dangerous a London fog can be to the lungs.'

'Like breathing in bed fluff,' said Slightly. And they agreed that the owner of the house must have closed the windows because clouds were rather like a London fog.

'Fly down the chimney, Fireflyer, and slip the bolt,' said Tootles, and the fairy swooped into the chimney pot. (Long years before it had been fashioned out of John's top hat, its crown pushed out, funnelling smoke into the sky.) They waited and waited, but when Tootles used one of her plaits to wipe a peephole in the dirt-caked windows, she could see that Fireflyer had got sidetracked and was swinging from a coat peg, eating the buttons off a jacket. 'Silly creature,' she said.

Wendy realized they must enter by a different route. 'You Lost Boys built the Wendy House,' she told them. 'You have a perfect right to take it apart again.' So, after knocking politely once more, they wrapped their fingers around the corner posts and wrenched off the end wall.

They were confronted by a boy, sword drawn, head tilted back and a ferocious scowl on his face. 'Have at you, Nightmares! You may breach my castle wall, but I shall fill up the gap with your dead bodies!' It was Peter Pan and it was not. His suit of skeleton leaves was gone, and in its place was a tunic of jay feathers and the blood-red leaves of autumn: Virginia creeper and maple.

'Now now, Peter,' said Wendy, stepping into the breach. 'Is that any way to greet your old friends?'

'*I have no friends who are old!*' cried the boy with the drawn sword. 'I am Boy and if things are big, I cut 'em down to size!'

Seeing that Peter did not recognize her, tears pricked behind Wendy's eyes, but she too tipped back her head. 'Don't be so silly,' she said briskly. 'You are Peter and I am Wendy, and we have come . . .'—she racked her brains trying to remember—'in case you were in trouble.'

Peter looked at her, baffled. 'How "in trouble"? In a cooking pot with cannibals waiting to eat me, you mean?'

'Well, maybe not that exactly . . .'

'Fallen off a ship in shark-infested waters?'

'Possibly not, but . . .'

'Being carried through the sky by a giant mother eagle to her eyrie to feed her hungry chicks?' It was plain Peter rather liked the idea of being in trouble. It was equally plain that none of these things were happening to him. Wendy began to feel rather foolish, which was something she never enjoyed.

'Have you been saying your prayers?' she demanded (a question every bit as scary as a sword waved in your face).

'Well, I haven't been saying anyone else's!' retorted Peter.

Then, for the first time, he looked at them properly. His sword-tip wavered and a great smile lit up his face. 'Ah. You've come back, then, have you? I thought I was dreaming you. I have dreamt you a lot, lately.' He added accusingly, 'You were *much too big*.'

The Twins hastily put back the wall, proving that they were not too big still to fit inside the Wendy House. 'How lucky you are, Peter! It must be first rate to live in the treetops! Did the fairies carry the house up here for you?'

'Not a bit of it,' said Peter. 'They wouldn't, the idle little brutes. They told people they had, but I did it all by myself!' (In actual fact, to set the records straight, it was the

Nevertree that did it. Peter had not troubled to cut the Nevertree level with the floor each morning. So it had simply grown and grown—clear up through the underground den and into the sunlight. One of its branches had scooped up the nearby Wendy House, lifting it higher than any other tree in the wood.) 'Why did you say you had come?'

'To do the Spring Cleaning, of course!' said Wendy, which was much simpler than explaining.

Carelessly Peter flung his sword into a corner. 'You can clean out the nightmares if you like,' he said.

Wendy was not exactly sure what Peter's nightmares looked like, so she swept down the black cobwebs from the corners of the ceiling. 'There! They are all gone now,' she said, and added breezily: 'We have been having nightmares, too. About Neverland. We thought something might be wrong.'

But either Peter did not know or he did not care about the dreams leaking out of Neverland: Neverland had dreams a-plenty to spare.

'Things outside look very ... *different*,' said Wendy carefully.

But of course Peter loved Neverland in scarlet and gold just as much as in summer greens, so he saw nothing wrong in that. Wendy did not press him. Perhaps she had been mistaken, and nothing was wrong.

'Are you quite well, Chief?' said Tootles tenderly, feeling Peter's pulse and the temperature of his forehead. 'If you are not, we can play doctors and nurses!'

'I am dying!' exclaimed Peter, throwing an arm across his face.

Wendy gave a cry of distress: 'Oh, I *knew* it! I *knew* something was wrong! I do hope you are not!'

'I am dying of boredom!' groaned Peter. Then he changed his mind and sprang to his feet. 'But now I have imagined you here, we can have the best adventures in the world!' And he uttered a triumphant crow that was thrilling and chilling and ear-splitting, all three:

'Cock-a-doodle-doo!'

And then he forgot they had ever been away. He did not notice that Tootles had become a girl or that Slightly could play the clarinet. Or that Nibs was missing.

Or Michael, for that matter.

'Is there no one else?' asked Wendy. 'No new Lost Boys? Or Girls?'

'I sent them away when they broke the Rules,' said Peter at once. 'Or killed them.' It was unlikely, but it made him sound marvellously ferocious. If any Lost Boys *had* found their way to the top of the Nevertree, they were not around now. For years, Peter Pan had been an only child—*the* only child—the One-and-Only Child in the Neverwood, with no one to keep him company but his shadow and the birds and the stars.

'Where's Tinker Bell?' asked Curly, looking in all the drawers. Peter only shrugged and said she had run off.

One visitor did catch his eye. He saw the puppy's head sticking out of Curly's pocket and said, 'You washed Nana and shrank her!' The last time he had seen the Darling children with a dog, it had been Nana, a gigantic Newfoundland dog who served for a nursemaid. The puppy wisely refrained from saying it was the great-great-great-grandpuppy of the wonderful Nana. It simply sat in the outstretched palms of the Wonderful Boy and licked off so much fairy dust, and thought such happy thoughts, that it floated up to the ceiling.

'Where's Tinker Bell?' asked the Twins, but Peter only shrugged and said he had turned her into a hornet because of her temper. Nobody believed that, either.

Peter held out the hilt of his sword. 'First you must all swear not to do any growing up.' And they all gave their solemn word. Then Peter declared them members of The League of Pan, adding, 'Tomorrow we shall go and do something dangerous and terrifically brave!'

Tootles folded her hands under her chin and her eyes shone. 'Oh yes, Peter! Do let's! Let's all go on a quest! We can call it Tootles's Quest, and everyone can go and find my heart's desire, and fight a deadly foe and one of you can win my hand!'

Peter stared at her. The plan had its merits, but it wasn't his. A tightness stiffened his little mouth. In the next second, his lips pursed and he gave the shrill whistle of a train about to leave—'All aboard!'

And at once the Wendy House was a carriage of the Trans-Sigobian Express, hurtling across desert and veldt with a cargo of bears and musical boxes and a patent mangle for the tsarina. It wobbled across rickety bridges over bottomless ravines. It plunged through mountain tunnels as dark as pitch. It was attacked by brigands and bounders, and once even by Baabaa-Rossa the sheepish Privateer. It out-raced Mongols and mughals riding mammoths. It drew up at a station staffed by ghosts in purple uniforms, who tried to eat the luggage. They drank Bovril from a samovar, and when John put a fishing rod out of the window, he reeled in a salmon as big as a horse. In an emergency (and there were lots), they leaned out of the window and pulled on the washing line to stop the train. It was Pretend, of course, but so exciting!

Make-believe worked its magic, Neverland cast its spell. The grown-ups who had set out from London full of good intentions, clean forgot why they had come: they were children again, and having far too much fun to worry about nightmares or misgivings or autumn in the Neverwood. They slept that night in the luggage racks of the Trans-

Sigobian Express, and the netting left criss-cross marks on their cheeks.

But John accidentally left the brake off at bedtime and when, hours later, the train rammed the buffers in Vladivostinopleburg, the Nevertree gave a shudder that loosened all the soil around its roots.

A dinner plate fell off a shelf in Grimswater. A baby cried in Fotheringdene.

The shock woke Wendy, and she lay for a while watching Fireflyer nibbling the laces out of his own little shoes. She thought again of Peter's fairy friend, Tinker Bell. How long do fairies live? As long as tortoises or as briefly as butterflies? Do they lose their wings in autumn and grow them again in spring? Or do they crumble like wasp's nests in winter? Surely not. Surely there *was* no winter in Neverland? In a whisper, she put the question to Fireflyer: 'How long do fairies live?'

And Fireflyer shouted, without a moment's thought or flicker of doubt, *'We live for ever, of course!'* It woke everyone up.

'Oh, you are *such* a whopping liar!' groaned Slightly drowsily, and Fireflyer grinned and bowed very low indeed.

Overnight, the clouds on the washing line had flapped themselves ragged and blown away. In their place hung black thunderclouds a-crackle with lightning. Beneath the Wendy House, the forest tossed and churned, and leaves spun past the windows.

Fearlessly, Peter skipped out along the branches to pick twigs for kindling, built a wonderful fire in the grate and lit it using nothing but the spark of Imagination. Then Wendy told them all such sensational sea stories that the Twins were seasick, and their imaginary midday milk tasted of rum. Outside, whole rookeries blew out of the treetops, but high in the storm-tossed Nevertree, the Twins declared they were 'ready to sail through waves as high as a house!' Curly said he would sail through waves as high as a hill. John said he would sail through waves as high as a mountain. Then everyone looked at Peter. He raised a fist over his head. 'I'd sail through waves as high as the MOOOOON!' he said. 'Then down to the bottom of the sea!'

At that, there was a noise like a ship's mast breaking, and the whole Wendy House lurched sideways. The League slid down the floor and piled up in a heap, along with the makings of the fire and Puppy, too. They clung to one another and tried to think happy thoughts so as to defy gravity. But it was hard as, one by one, they realized: the whole Nevertree was listing, toppling, swooning . . . *FALLING*.

As it fell, the tree fumbled its grip on the Wendy House, which spun out into empty air, floor over roof over window. Branches impaled its walls; boughs caught it, then instantly broke and let it fall further, a spinning box full of falling figures plunging towards the forest floor. John had the presence of mind to pull the communication cord . . .

But it did not stop them crashing to the ground.

Chapter Five
Tootles's Quest

Thanks to the storm, a million leaves had fallen to the forest floor ahead of the Wendy House. The splash sounded like water, but water would have been harder. They sank and sank, then sprang up again from the spongy mattress of twigs, leaves, and old bird's nests. It was impossible to see what damage had been done, for down here among the undergrowth there was barely any light. Only the glimmer of Fireflyer, darting angrily about, lightened the ton of dark weighing down on them. The League of Pan picked themselves up and wondered what to do. Wendy called everyone to her and checked them over for injuries. There were only a few scratches and bruises and torn clothes.

She thought, when she stumbled over Peter, that he was worse hurt: there was a trickle of blood coming from his nose. Quickly she pulled out the handkerchief from her sleeve and tried to staunch the flow, but he jerked his head away and glowered. 'Don't touch me! I mustn't be touched!' That was when she realized: he was sulking hugely. 'Now see what you've done, all of you. I said you were too big! Now look. You have smashed my house! I wish you had never come!'

'It was the storm, Peter!' said Wendy; though she had not been hurt by the fall, her heart hurt now.

'I was better on my own,' grunted the Only Child.

The Nevertree lay along the ground, its roots bleeding gouts of earth. The storm mumbled on. On several of the tree trunks, posters advertised:

But the corners were curling and the paper was peeling as the paste failed in the rain. Somewhere the puppy was barking, though the where of it seemed to be somewhere else. Their whistles and shouts fetched only hoots, growls, and hisses from the undergrowth: wild things were prowling the Neverwood, with eyes that could see better than theirs in the dark.

'I can hear Puppy!' said a Twin. 'Somewhere underneath us!'

'I do believe it has found our dear old den!' said the other.

'MY den!' barked Peter. 'I just don't use it any more.'

By following the unhappy sound of the puppy, they found their way to the circle of toadstools that marked Peter Pan's underground den, and clambered about trying to remember how to get in. Years before, each had entered by sliding down their own particular hollow tree. Tootles found *her* tree, but found, too, that she did not fit it; she had become a slightly different shape since the faraway days of Before. The others twisted and turned her—'*Oh, mind my frock!*'—this way and that—'*Ow, mind my plaits!*'—trying to post her down the chute. '*Ouch, mind my moustache!*'

'Tootles, you haven't *got* a moustache!'

Down below, the puppy's barking grew frantic. *Something* had taken up home in the underground chamber: a badger? a python? a giant truffle? Whatever it was, Puppy had a very low opinion of it. In fact, as Tootles struggled to get down, the puppy was trying to get up, so that neither could manage. The Something began to stir and move about.

'So *that's* why you don't live down there any more!' said Slightly, edging backwards, shivering in his evening shirt and bare legs.

'Don't care to!' Peter retorted. 'Could kill it if I wanted, but I liked living up in the treetops . . . until you all came along and broke my house!'

Peter's sulk cast a guilty gloom over everyone. They shuffled their feet and picked at the circus posters on the trees, tried to warm their palms round Fireflyer, and glanced towards Wendy for help.

'Soon, can we go to the circus?' said John.

'Ooo, can we, Peter? Can we?' begged the Twins. 'We'd be out of the rain!'

'And there might be clowns!'

'I hate clowns,' said Peter. 'You can't see what they're thinking.'

Around them, the trees could be heard clenching their roots in the ground, cracking their knuckles. It was impossible to tell what the trees were thinking, either.

'As soon as it's light,' said Wendy, 'we shall build a new home!' and everyone felt instantly brighter . . . except for the One-and-Only-Child. Perhaps Adventure was calling him, or perhaps he had grown too used to making all the decisions.

'No we shan't!' he said, tossing Wendy's bloodstained handkerchief aside. 'Why stay at home? We shall all go on a Quest!' He said it as if no one in the whole history of the world had ever spoken the words before or had such a wonderful idea.

'Oh, a Quest, yes!' said Tootles, entranced. 'What a cracking idea!'

'I can't help it. I'm just so marvellously clever,' Peter explained. 'Anyway, the Quester who brings Princess Tootles the heart of a dragon wins her hand, and a Happy Never After!'

'Dragon?' said Tootles, startled, and scratched her top lip.

Wendy looked sternly at Peter, thinking there had already been enough danger for one night.

'But it's raining!' said a Twin.

'Then we shall get wet!' said Peter.

'And muddy!' cried Curly.

'And mucky!'

That clinched it. Adventure and the chance to get dirty were calling too loud to ignore.

The Twins said they would go questing together and share the prize (since Tootles had two hands). Slightly asked if he could win half a kingdom instead of Tootles's hand. Curly started to say that he couldn't win Tootles's hand because he was already married, but broke off, for that was clearly nonsense and he could not imagine what had put such an idea into his head.

Fireflyer said that he was too hungry to go questing anywhere, and began scouting about for conkers to eat. When the top-hat chimney suddenly came rattling down out of the tree-canopy, he took shelter inside it, out of the rain. The Questers snatched up dead wood to use for swords.

'Off you go now!' urged Tootles delightedly. 'I'll count to twenty!' and she turned her face to a tree and covered her eyes. The Questers waded away waist-deep through the fallen leaves, towards all points of the compass.

'When I come back,' said Peter to Wendy, in a low voice, 'I shall build a stockade and call it Fort Pan. Those others can't come in, because they broke my house. But you can, if you like.' He said it as if he did not greatly care one way or the other. 'You stay here with Tootles while I go questing.'

'Nonsense!' said Wendy. 'I want to go questing too! I don't much want Tootles's hand, but I've never seen a dragon!'

Princess Tootles, after counting to twelve-ish, picked up the top hat with Fireflyer in it, and struggled out of the wood. She sheltered from the rain in the mouth of a cave, at the head of a beach, and made herself a throne out of seaweed, a crown out of some pretty pieces of metal she found lying about. 'I dub you Royal Liar Extraordinary!' she told Fireflyer and he was so flattered that his scorching little body set the seaweed pop-pop-popping.

Dawn welled up, and Tootles glimpsed the shifting, oily sheen of the Lagoon. In her memory, it had been a shining crescent of turquoise water over shoals of white sand. The Lagoon she saw now was darkly heaving: a horse's flank slick black and streaked with foam. A mane of washed-up seaweed lay among the pebbles, busy with flies. All along the high-water mark lay strange, white containers, like birdcages or crab-pots. On closer inspection they proved to be the skeleton ribcages of mermaids, with here and there a backbone or a hank of yellow hair. Tootles looked nervously around and ran back to the cave.

Meanwhile, the Twins found a Forest Dragon, with wooden limbs and a wooden body and a sharp, spiky mane of twigs. Just like a pile of fallen trees, in fact. They killed it with fire.

At about mid-morning, Slightly spotted a Cloud Dragon. It filled the sky from one horizon to another . . . until the wind sprang up and it went all to pieces.

At about midday, Curly reached a beach and found a Water Dragon. Every few seconds, the Dragon surged up the beach towards him, shapeless and smelling of salt, then retreated again. Curly tried to kill it, but his blade went straight through its watery hide and his boots got wet. So he sat down on the beach and threw stones at it instead.

In the mid-afternoon, John sighted a Rock Dragon: knobbly spine of limestone, a boulder of a head, and a pebbly cascade of tail. John left his wooden sword sticking up out of its neck. A triumph, he told himself.

Meanwhile, Wendy could not think where to look for a dragon. Surely they do not live in the open, she thought, or people would see them all the time and take photographs. Then she glimpsed one—its shoulder, at least—a great bulging thing the colour of blood, rising up from behind a hill. Her heart tried to jump out of her mouth but got wedged. She wanted to whistle up Peter, but her lips were too dry to blow. Wendy shut her eyes tight. Only as she crawled closer on hands and knees did she remember that she had not made herself a sword. The dragon rattled horribly loud—obviously a saggy, baggy monster with loose, flapping skin . . . And so big!

When she finally dared to open her eyes, Wendy burst out laughing. Not a dragon at all—just a huge, wind-blown circus tent! She could read the word

RAVELLO

painted in fading letters across the canvas roof. Ship's cables tethered it to the ground. Around the tent were various cages on wheels, some empty, some with zebras or ostriches inside; a gorilla, three tigers, and a cotillo; a puma, an okapi, and a palmerion. None of the cage doors were shut. Ponies with plumes in their browbands grazed the grass round about. From inside the tent came the strains of a piano. Intrigued, Wendy climbed down for a closer look.

It was not a proper piano, at all, but a pianola, reading its music off a paper roll. The keys dipped, though no fingers were touching them, and a carved wooden figure on top of the lid conducted the music in jerky movements, squeaking for want of oil. Wendy was so eager to see it close up that she ducked indoors. The air glowed yellow and the noise of the wind was thunderous in the big hollow space. There was a smell of cough drops and damp sheep.

Oh, and a hint of lion.

Wendy had reached the centre of the sawdust floor before she saw them. They were ranged around the tent like the numbers round the face of a clock: twelve lions seated on upturned tin baths.

'Ah!' said a voice behind her. 'A customer.' It was a low, soft voice, plush as velvet, with sibilants as swashing as the sea. 'Welcome to Circus Ravello. I was so hoping you would come.' The lions rumbled like thunder. 'Your devoted servant, madam. Do pray stand still, or my cat-kins may mistake you for lunch.'

Against the brightness of the doorway, the speaker was a patch of darkness in a halo of daylight. His outline was frizzed. Wendy could just make out a prodigious garment of some kind, its sleeves reaching far beyond the finger-ends, the hem straggling to the very welts of his shineless boots: a thousand broken strands of wool, coiling and kinking, blurred the bounds between man and shadow. There was no telling where his wild hair ended and the hooded cardigan began. The colour of both had unravelled, too. A sheep tangled in barbed wire would have looked a lot like this tangle of manhood. And yet he moved with feline grace, planting his feet one in front of the other like a tightrope walker crossing a ravine.

'I did so hope you would come,' he said again. 'My heart rejoices at it. My creatures and I are honoured by your kindness.' The voice trickled into her like golden syrup into a steamed pudding. Coils of bushy, shineless hair and the woollen hood encroached over the face, but she could make out a pair of large, hazel eyes watching her as attentively as the lions were doing. 'Come,' he said extending a woolly arm towards her. 'Walk slowly towards me and make no sudden motion. My cat-kins have not eaten today. Above all, do not—you will forgive the indelicacy of a vulgar animal trainer—do not, whatever you do, *sweat*. Sweat, you see, falls sharp in the nostrils of a hungry cat-kin.' His voice poured like hot chocolate over vanilla ice cream. Even the lions' ears swivelled to catch it. Clawed paws shifted on twelve tin baths, with a noise like scouring saucepans.

Wendy, as she stepped closer to the lion tamer, could see how every hem and seam and raglan of the shapeless cardigan was unravelling. Moth holes peppered the fabric, and every moth hole had also begun to unravel. He was a woolly miasma of trailing ends.

'I am Miss Wendy Darling,' she said, reaching out to shake hands (though the man's hands were quite invisible). If she could make friends with their master, the lions might stop thinking of her as lunch.

The pale brown eyes wrinkled as if her name alone had bestowed the greatest joy. 'And I am Ravello, owner of this lamentably humble establishment. I feel certain you will do better with your life than I have with mine.' He reached forward, too, and Wendy found her hand full of the ravelling cuff of his over-long sleeve. 'Tell me, child, what is it you wish to be when you are *grown-up?*'

'I—' But before Wendy could answer, a blood-curdling scream scattered her thoughts and filled her outstretched palm with sweat. 'Tootles! That's Tootles!' she gasped and darted past the circus master and out of the tent. Her only thought was to rescue Tootles from danger. Behind her she heard twelve tin baths overturn and Ravello's voice sharp and loud, trying to quell the lions. But she only ran and ran.

At the head of a beach was a cave and out of the mouth of the cave came Tootles's voice shrieking, 'DRAAAAHAAAGON!'

Bored with waiting for her questing knights to come back, Tootles had begun to explore the cave. The darkness dripped. Lovely shells glistened in pools on the floor, and the walls were furry with cold, green slime. Deeper in, though, there was no colour and no gleam—only the drip-drip of water like the topmost note of a piano played over and over again. A low roof banged her on the head and knocked her crown over one ear. Soon she had to explore with fingertips, because there was no light at all. And that was when her outstretched hand felt the knobbly hide, the snout, the row of ghastly teeth that went on and on and . . . Tootles gave a gurgling shriek 'DRAAAAHAAAGON!'— and ran. The low ceiling caught her on the head again and this time it knocked her crown to pieces.

The echoes of her scream died away. Plink plink said the tone-deaf darkness. Then a grip fastened on one shoulder, and her knees crumpled with fright as she was spun round.

'Tell me where and I'll slay it dead!' said a voice close to her ear. It was Peter, a blazing driftwood torch in his hand. One by one, the rest of Pan's League appeared at his back. 'Where?' said Peter again. Tootles pointed wordlessly, and the League streamed past him while she stayed rooted to the spot, fingers absently stroking her top lip. Last to arrive, Wendy gave her a caring pat and galloped on by to catch up with the boys.

And there it was—an eye socket, a gaping jaw, a snaggle of teeth as long as a man's arm. 'Stand back, men!' cried Pan and lunged with his sword and rapped it over the skull, then sprang backwards expecting it to scuttle out of its lair, jaws snapping. In the jumping firelight from their torches, the monster appeared to shudder and writhe . . . but when John threw a rock at it, the rock only knocked out a rattle of teeth.

Then Fireflyer darted in through one eye socket and out of the other, illuminating the grisly skull. *'Nothing in here!'* he complained, peering up at the skull like a tourist at a cathedral roof. The dragon was dead.

Peter put a hand through its nostril and together they dragged it out into the daylight. It was monstrous big. When all the Lost Boys lay down end to end, they were not as long as the dead dragon from snout to tail. They rolled it on its back and found that the stomach hide was gone altogether, leaving only a ladder of ribs and a glimpse of backbone. There was a smell of rotting fish, mermaid, and, oddly enough, gunpowder.

'I win!' said Peter. 'I quested the dragon!'

'Superb!' exclaimed Tootles.

' *'Tain't a dragon,'* said Fireflyer, still sitting on the snout. Peter launched a kick at him, but he ducked. *'Well, it ain't! Dragons've got fireproof tonsils. Everyone knows that! This here's a nalligator.'*

' 'Tis NOT a nalligator!' insisted Tootles, who was delighted that Peter had won her hand. 'Take no notice. That fairy is always lying.'

'Nalligator or not,' said Curly, holding his nose, 'it's awfully dead.'

'Not a nalligator,' muttered Tootles under her breath.

'Now now, boys,' said Wendy soberly. 'Don't quarrel. All that matters is that . . .'

'Not a nalligator,' said Tootles sulkily, several times over.

Wendy noticed something shiny dangling from Tootles's hair and pulled it free. It was a metal spring. Tootles explained how she had found the makings of a crown inside the cave.

Wendy nodded sagely. 'This one time,' she said, 'Fireflyer is telling the truth. It is not a nalligator . . .'

'Told you!' crowed Peter. 'It's a dragon!'

'I never tell the truth!' protested Fireflyer (which was not true, of course).

'Nor a dragon!' said Wendy, holding up the spring. 'It is

a crocodile. In fact, it is THE Crocodile, with capital letters! The one who ate our direst foe. Here, dear Boys, in Tootles's crown, you see all that remains of the alarm clock it carried in its stomach as it hunted Neverland, looking for a bite more of Captain James Hook!'

The very mention of Hook sent a thrilling shiver down their spines. Curly felt the curls in his curly hair tighten. For though they had witnessed the end with their own eyes— had seen the pirate captain leap to his death in the jaws of a gigantic crocodile, Captain Jas. Hook still had the power to haunt their dreams. They gazed down at the carcass in awe, and the jaws grinned smugly back at them.

'So has *anybody* won my hand?' moaned Princess Tootles, determined that *someone* must have.

'I found a stone dragon!' said John. 'They're the worst!'

'I found a cloud dragon,' said Slightly.

'A water dragon, me,' said Curly, unlacing his wet shoes.

'Ours was made of wood,' said the Twins, 'and we killed it with fire!'

'I found twelve lions,' said Wendy mildly, 'though I don't suppose that counts.'

Peter simply kicked the Crocodile. A hinge in the cheek broke, and the top jaw slowly lifted. It even seemed as if smoke coiled out, but it was only mist rolling off the Lagoon. The weather was certainly strange: it is rare to be dazzled by lightning and tickled by mist in the same night.

'You all did very well,' said Wendy, seeing trouble brewing. 'Would you like to hear about my lions now? And the Circus?'

'Well, we can't *share*,' said Curly. 'You can't *share* a princess. How would you split her up?'

Peter fingered his dagger, at which Tootles looked distinctly uneasy.

'There are lots of different days in the week,' said Wendy brightly. 'Perhaps Tootles could lend you a hand on Wednesday, Slightly, and you a hand on Thursday . . .'

'I'd rather have half a kingdom anyway,' said Slightly.

'Well, you can't,' said John, 'because I quested best and killed a stone dragon and they're the worst!' The Boys began to bump and barge each other. Even the Twins started a fight over which of them had set light to the Forest Dragon.

'Let's have a story,' said Wendy quickly.

Peter leapt on to a big rock. 'No! Let's have a WAR!'

This marvellous idea of his set Fireflyer whooping and wheeling in fits of delight. *'A war, yes! I never saw a war!'* The fairy clung to Peter's unkempt hair, like fire to a fuse.

The Twins stopped fighting. John brushed sand off his sailor suit.

'No,' said Wendy. 'Don't let's.'

'No,' said Curly. 'Let's not.'

'No,' said John. 'Not a War.'

Perhaps it was the clammy touch of the mist. Perhaps it was the ghost of a memory. Perhaps, in far off Fotheringdene someone leaned against the war memorial on the village green . . .

'Done War,' said one Twin.

'Me too,' said the other.

'Michael wouldn't like it,' said Slightly.

Peter stamped his foot in outrage. 'And just *who* is *Michael*?'

John gave a gasp. Wendy turned away. Could Peter really have forgotten their brother? Their wonderful brother Michael? For a long time no one spoke. There was only the noise of Fireflyer fizzing and fretting around their heads.

'Michael Darling went away to the Big War,' said Slightly. 'He was . . . Lost.'

Peter stared at them, these mutineers, with their white faces, wet hair, sad eyes. Then he somersaulted carelessly off the rock. 'Ah! One of the Lost Boys! Do you expect me to remember them all? There were so many!'

No one tried to explain. They knew that Peter Pan (and foolish young fairies like Fireflyer) were much better off *not* knowing about the War. Besides, something else had put it quite out of their heads.

Five large black bears, jaws agape and slavering, were leaping towards them over the rocks.

CHAPTER SIX

A Ravelling Man

'*Hup, cub-bages!*' said a deep, imperious voice.

The bears lurched up on to their haunches, roaring, rolling their black heads on their thick no-necks, drooling saliva and dancing in waltz-time: one-two-three; one-two- three.

Peter Pan spread wide his arms: he would shield his League from harm or die in the attempt! Behind the bears, out of the wreathing mist, came a sixth shape, almost as tall, almost as shaggy. There was a crack like gunfire.

'*Wet your whistles, cub-bages!*' said the Great Ravello, coiling up his long, rawhide whip. The bears dropped down, long claws sinking like grappling irons into the soft sand, and lumbered down to the water's edge to drink. 'Gentlemen . . . ladies. I hope my little pets did not scare you.'

'Fear is a stranger to me!' declared Peter, hands on hips.

'Two strangers met in one day, then, Peter Pan,' said the circus-master. 'Fear and Myself.'

Peter was startled. 'You know my name?'

Ravello came closer, his woolly garment dragging, erasing his own light footprints. His voice was softer even than the sand. 'Naturally I know you, Peter Pan. Who has not heard of the Marvellous Boy? The Boy from Treetops? The Fearless Avenger! The Wonder of Neverwood! The flame of your fame lights my every dull day. You are the stuff of legend!'

The League of Pan gave a rousing cheer, except for Wendy, who thought so many compliments might go to Peter's head. Sure enough, Pan gave a shrill crow of pleasure:

'Cock-a-doodle-doo!'

The bears in the surf jerked upright and rocked from foot to foot, rattling their claws like dinner knives.

'Ah, I must caution against loud noises,' urged the circus- master, in tones so sweet that the bears, sniffing the air, scented honey. 'My cub-bages are nervous of loud noises. They might run amok.'

Curly, watching the bears with a mixture of terror and fascination, asked if they really ought to be drinking from the Lagoon. 'I read somewhere: doesn't drinking seawater make you go mad?'

'Pray do not fret on their account, young man. They are all stark mad already.' Seeing Wendy, the circus-master bowed deeply from the waist—'We meet once more, Miss Wendy. Your servant, ma'am. Your most humble servant,'—then addressed himself again to Peter. 'I might likewise ask if it is wise for people of tender age to be out so late. Please tell me you have the prospect of warm beds and a filling supper?' When they said they did not, he at once invited them to return with him to the Circus Ravello. 'In these lean and hungry times many of my cages are empty. They are clean and mattressed with soft, fresh hay. I would deem it an honour . . .'

'We don't go about with grown-up people,' Peter interrupted, scuffing his foot in the sand.

'Oh. Very well. But you will at least come to the Circus, won't you?' persisted Ravello. 'I bring tickets for you, look! Tickets for the circus? Everyone loves an outing to the circus! Clowns and acrobats? Bears, tigers, lions! Jugglers! Escapologists? Illusionists. Bare-back riders! A flying trapeze . . . !' And he pulled from somewhere a deck of scarlet tickets that he fanned out before flicking them high in the air to fall like autumn leaves over the children's heads.

'Oh yes, Peter! A circus!' Tootles was not the only one whose face lit up at the thought.

'Nor we don't choose to sleep in cages neither!' said Peter.

'. . . thank you all the same,' Wendy added hastily.

Ravello did not seem to take offence. 'Have you never dreamed . . . Has none of you ever dreamed of joining a circus—of running away to a five-ring life of gasps and laughter and cheering? Picture it! Dancing with the raggle-taggle gypsies to the quacking of trombones! Hearts thumping in time with the thud of hoofbeats on sawdust! The flash of lamplight on sequinned leotards?' There was an awkward pause, during which Ravello looked from child to child with his oddly eager gaze.

The puppy was the only one who moved towards him, and that was to sniff the curious frizz that wrapped the circus master from head to foot. It pounced on a trailing bundle of ravelled wool and was instantly tangled up, so that Curly had to hurry over and try to free it. His own fingers got embarrassingly snagged somewhere between the man's knobbly, mottled boots. Ravello looked down at him patiently with eyes the colour of an English sea. 'You show a great concern for animals, young man. Do you see yourself as a veterinary man, perhaps? One day? When you are older?'

'I—'

Puppy suddenly and unkindly nipped the circus-master,

so that he gave a cry of pain. It startled the bears and brought them romping up the beach, black noses drizzling, black eyes beady bright. A dead fish dangled from one mouth, a crab from another. They stood up tall, to push between the children, towering over them, at least twice their height, great shawls of gleaming fur brushing bare little arms.

'Gently, my furry furies,' breathed Ravello. 'No dancing tonight. We are not wanted here.' And hunching his clothing closer around him, he turned to go, the tail of his rawhide whip trailing snake-like through the sand. The bears dropped on to all fours to trot after him.

'Who are you?' called Slightly. He was sensitive to hurt feelings and could smell them as surely as lions can smell sweat, or bears honey.

Ravello turned. 'Me? Oh, just a travelling man,' he said. 'A simple travelling man. But I will not impose myself upon you any longer, since you find no need of me or mine. I must go now: feed my beasts and master my disappointment. I had *hoped* to be of service to the Marvellous Boy. But alas, Hope is nothing but a cruel trick practised upon us by the gods. Goodnight, gentlemen . . . ladies.' The mist closed behind him like the doors of a cathedral and the only sound left was the hissing surf of a turning tide.

The Twins bent to gather up the tickets, but Peter snatched them and tore them all in shreds. 'We don't need grown-ups!' he said. 'We are all right as we are!' and his face brooked no argument.

'He might have given us egg and toast soldiers for supper. that ravelling man,' said Fireflyer unwisely, and Peter swatted him into a rock pool.

'*Travelling* man,' Wendy corrected Fireflyer, pulling him out again and drying him in the skirts of her dress. 'Not "ravelling".'

'Perhaps he's not a grown-up,' suggested Tootles. 'You couldn't really see, could you? Maybe he's just a big one of us.'

'Or a very tall cardigan,' said John nodding.

But Peter refused to listen. The thought of sleeping in a cage (whether or not the straw was dry) struck horror into his freewheeling soul. The thought of animals caged was almost as bad. It appalled him to think of wild creatures penned up behind bars. It was almost as if they were trapped inside him—those bears and tigers and lions— pacing up and down, pushing their plush noses between the bars of his ribcage, so that he wanted to tear open his chest and set them all free . . . A terrible foreboding settled over his heart, which he did not understand. And not understanding always gave Peter a pain.

'Well, where *are* we going to sleep tonight?' whinged Princess Tootles.

'Peter, do you smell smoke?' said Wendy.

Peter lifted his face and his nostrils flared. 'Signal fires,' he said. 'Or bonfires . . . Maybe the Tribes are feasting.' But over the sound of the sea washed a different kind of noise, like a giant moaning in her sleep and turning over on a mattress of brittle straw. Crackling. There were the cries of animals, too: frightened, agitated animals. It was impossible to tell whether the mist was growing thicker or just meshing with the smoke. Certainly the smoke was thick enough now to make the children cough.

'About that Forest Dragon of yours, Twins . . .' began Peter. 'How did you say you killed it?'

'With fire. Why? Oh. Oh!'

Now the Neverwood began to glow, showing its bones, showing the tilt, this way and that, of dead trees. Something monstrous was coming through the woods, and this time it was not a covey of bears or a dragon or the Trans-Sigobian Express.

It was Fire.

A ghostly, billowing shape broke clear of the treetops and rose into the night sky trailing a dozen fuses. It glowed orange, being full of fire. And written quite clearly across it was the word

RAVELLO

The circus tent, its guy ropes blazing, kept on rising until, crumpling into a ball of flame, it lost its shape and fell back down into the general inferno.

'Oh, Twins! What have you done!' whispered Tootles.

'Slayed a dragon is all!' protested the Twins.

Somewhere, inside that blazing forest, was the wreckage of the Wendy House, the Underground Den, several cages full of dry, clean straw, and a circus-master clad in a garment of ravelling wool. The Neverwood filled up with the cries of lynxes and lions, zebras and gorillas, tigers and palmerions. Sparks began to rain out of the sky, as if the stars were falling piecemeal.

'Time to go,' said Peter as the heat reached them on the beach, and the Lagoon began to steam.

But where to go? They were trapped—penned in between the burning forest and the sea. The Neverwood was smudged out. The cave had melted from sight. Without them noticing, the misty smoke and smoky mist had grown so thick that they could barely see further than each other.

So they all turned to face the Lagoon. And out of the Lagoon, as though summoned by trumpets, came the most startling sight of all. Their sore eyes grew wide as wide. John's lips shaped the blessed words:

'Sail ho!'

CHAPTER SEVEN

A Certain Coat

'Sail ho!' he shouted, feet rising from the ground in exultation.

Through the moiling yellow smoke came the bowsprit of a ship, like a dueller's sword—*en garde!* Behind it, the fat black bow of a brig that has fed deep on adventure, shouldering aside the oil-black waves. A dank, flapping noise spoke of slack black sails and the snaking ends of free-flying ropes. With a soft grinding of gravel and sand, the keel touched bottom and the ship shuddered from end to end, angry that mere dry land should have got in its way. Adrift in the mist, the *Jolly Roger* had simply run out of sea.

She stood now, prow upraised in a haughty sneer, daring the little waves jumping and barking around her ankles to make a nuisance of themselves.

'I know this ship!' said Peter, and so did they all. For even those whose reading was not good enough to tackle the name on the bow could make out the skull-and-crossbones lolling at the masthead.

'It's HIS ship!' breathed Slightly.

They waited for the rumble of cannon being run out. They listened for the cry from the deck of 'Avast, ye swabs!' But the beached ship was silent except for the creak of timbers groaning, *Aground! Aground!*

Peter was first aboard, of course, climbing up by way of the barnacles and the gun ports, calling for the rest to follow. 'What are you afraid of? Hook's dead and gone, isn't he? Over there's the Crocodile that ate him!'

Tootles and Slightly followed, but the littler boys hung back, remembering how they had been prisoners once aboard this ship—lashed to the mast—sentenced to walk the plank. Even with the forest fire raging at their backs and nothing but smoke to breathe, it took Wendy to shame them into moving. She clambered up after Peter singing a sea shanty as she went.

She tried not to say, even to herself, how fearful it was to walk the decks, to climb the companionways, to tug open cabin doors and look inside. Now and then a shadowy figure would suddenly loom out of the choking murk, and utter a shout and reach for its sword. Then the mist would shift and there stood Curly or John or Slightly, head forward, peering, trembling with fright because *they* had just seen *her* shadowy shape. Curly fell over a cannon; Slightly walked into the ship's bell which clanged like the knell of doom. When the smoke momentarily cleared, and moonlight poured down, the mast looked so tall you might climb up it with a candlesnuffer and put out all the stars.

Everything was exactly as it had been the night oh-so-long-before when Peter Pan and the villainous pirate Captain Hook had fought to the death over who should keep Wendy for a mother. Since then, spiders had woven webs between the spokes of the ship's-wheel. Rust had caked the cannon balls to their racks. Rats had bred and raised young and grown old and retired to barns in the countryside. Seagulls had whitened the sails, and rain had washed them black again. But no rope-soled shoes or high-cuffed boots had walked the quarterdeck for twenty years. No songs had sounded in the fo'c'sle; no bo'sun's pipe had whistled anyone aboard the *Jolly Roger*. She was a ghostly ship adrift on a ghostly ocean, damp and dank and dead.

But to homeless adventurers needing to escape the beach—out late and in want of somewhere to sleep—it was a wish come true. Hammocks still hung between the bulkheads. There were ship's biscuits in the biscuit barrels and Christmas puddings in the brandy barrels and fresh rain in the water butts. There were boots in the footlockers and several kitbags, too, labelled **Smee**, **Starkey**, **Cecco**, **Jukes** . . .

'How long do pirates live, do you think?' asked Curly.

And there was a sea chest.

Wendy aired the fo'c'sle as she aired her opinions, for just the right length of time, then tucked up the Boys in their hammocks and set them swinging.

There were charts in the chartroom, signal flags and oilskins, a telescope for looking-out, and a compass for steering by. There was a kettle and cocoa, and something white in the powder kegs that would do for flour—or talcum powder in a crisis.

And there was the sea chest.

J. H. it said on the lid, which opened like a cupboard and had drawers inside for socks, lace collars, and medals. There was a brass telescope as heavy as a gun. There was another brass instrument with slides and calibrations and knurled knobs of no known usefulness. There was a frock coat in red brocade and, coiled in a corner like a pale snake, a white tie or cravat. Peter Pan put on the coat, admired his reflection in the speckled cabin mirror, then pocketed the telescope and climbed the mainmast to the crow's nest. Cracking the tie like a whip, he tipped back his head and crowed so loudly that the stars blinked.

'Cock-a-doodle-doo!

'I shall be Captain Peter Pan, and sail the seven oceans!' he shouted, and dislodged an albatross roosting on the mizzenmast.

Back on deck, Wendy had to knot the tie for him: he had never worn a man's tie round his throat before. 'I believe you'll find there are seven seas but only five oceans,' she said as she did so. Peter sank his hands into the deep pockets of the red brocade coat. There were holes in the lining where a pirate's pieces-of-eight might easily fall through; this must be Hook's second-best coat. Well, of course it was! The best one had slithered, together with its owner, down the Crocodile's throat. 'Stand still and don't fidget,' said Wendy sternly (because tying a gentleman's tie takes time and skill).

But Peter had found something else in his pocket, other than holes. Between his fingers he felt the crumbly softness of finest vellum chart-paper. 'Look here! Look what I've found!' he cried, waving the chart over his head. 'A treasure map! And here's where Hook stowed his treasure!'

Out of a landscape of cream vellum rose forests and hills, lighthouses and mountains. And there, sure enough, like a teacher's angry crossing-out, a big black **X** had been gouged through the highest mountain of all. '**Neverpeak**' read the inky scrawl underneath.

'Wind the capstans and man the yards!' cried Peter. 'Clear the decks and make ready!' and if he was startled to find such sea-salty words in his mouth, he did not show it.

Heads popped up through every hatch. 'What? Why? Where are we going?'

'Yes,' said Wendy fretfully, 'where are we going? There will be so much tidying up to do after the fire.'

'We're going on a voyage of discovery!' cried Peter. 'We're going in search of treasure!'

'A treasure hunt!' The cry was taken up by everyone. 'A treasure hunt!' A treasure hunt, across uncharted waters, round the island and ashore again in unknown territories— along the untrodden paths of Neverland and into the unimagined dangers of Never-been-there-land! All thoughts but these—all plans but this—melted from the minds of Pan's comrades.

Even the ocean felt the surge of excitement— TREASURE!—for it fairly rushed into the bay. The tide came in much faster than it does on unremarkable days. It refloated the *Jolly Roger* and spun her round so that her bowsprit pointed out to sea—*en garde!* Peter's trusty crew swarmed into the rigging, hoping that, from up there, they would be able to see over the horizon. Sparks from the burning forest swarmed around their heads and brushed the canvas sails. Not a moment too soon, they left the Bay of Dragons behind them and sailed into the night. As they crossed the bar, and a salt spray wetted their faces, even the ship seemed caught up by the splendour of the enterprise, for at midnight the ship's bell rang eight times.

And no one was anywhere near it.

CHAPTER EIGHT
All at Sea

The *Jolly Roger*, after so long without a crew, answered eagerly to the smallest turn of the ship's helm. Peter cut such a dash in his scarlet frock coat (once the sleeves were shortened) that the League of Pan would have walked on water to please him. Here and there along the coast, he took them ashore to forage for breadfruit, and for butternuts and honeycomb to spread on it. He rigged awnings out of sails, where they could shelter when it rained. He gave them ranks—Rear Admiral, Front Admiral, First Sea Lord, Other Sea Lord, Best Mate, Deckmaster, Mastmaster, and Keeper of the Crow's Nest. He told them: 'I'll stick by you for ever and lay down my life for you, if you'll join my Company of Explorers!'—And they would have sworn on their sword hilts if they had had any proper swords.

Sometimes the ferocity of his orders took them by surprise, but it was worth it to serve in such a happy crew. His cleverness at sailing a ship astonished them. The names of obscure ropes and bits of rigging came to him in an instant. He even knew how to curse like a sailor.

'That's *quite* enough of that, thank you,' said Wendy.

For hours, he would sit at the chart desk in Hook's stateroom at the stern of the vessel, and write up the ship's log using a raven's feather, dipping it into a china flagon of blood red ink. Since he had never learned to read or write, he filled the pages with pictures instead of words, recording the day's events.

Then he would return to poring over Hook's treasure map, wondering what had taken the villain so far from the sea carrying a heavy treasure chest, what booty Hook had taken such pains to stash away? What hardships would face explorers who went in search of it?

He changed the brig's name, of course—to the *Jolly Peter*—and refused to sail under the pirate flag. 'I am no scurvy brigand to fly the skull-and-crossbones!' he told Wendy. 'Make me a flag, girl!'

'What's the little word that gets things done?' said Wendy, who was a stickler for good manners.

Peter racked his brains. Having had no mother to teach him manners, he had no idea what the little word might be. 'Button?' he suggested. 'Thimble? Flag?'

Wendy smiled, kissed him lightly on the cheek, and went to make a flag out of her sundress, a dress out of the pirate flag. So it was under the emblem of sunflower-and-two rabbits that the *Jolly Peter* sailed through the Straits of Zigzag and the Widego Narrows and into the Sea of One Thousand Islands. Flying fish leapt over the ship and diving gulls plunged under it, resurfacing with beaks full of whitebait.

The Thousand Islands came in all shapes and sizes. There were rocks only fit to strand a sailor on; desert islands with one palm tree and some coconut matting; mangrove islands noisy with parrots; archipelagos of red coral and archipelouses strewn with fine, green lawns. There were extinct volcanic atolls, and islands not at all extinct whose volcanoes smoked and rumbled and tossed lumps of molten rock far out to sea. There were islands shaped like turtles and others shaped simply like islands but teeming with turtles. All these Peter found marked on the charts, as well as lighthouses and headlands, whirlpools and estuaries. In the shaded areas labelled '**Fishing Grounds**' a magnet swung over the side would bring in a can of sprats or a tin of sardines. There were wrecks, and drowned villages whose church bells rang when the sea was rough . . .

It vexed Peter that the islands that passed by the casement windows of his cabin looked nothing like the ones on the charts. Stupidly the chart-makers had drawn everything as if they were looking down on it from above: all very well if you are travelling by hot-air balloon but confusing to a ship's captain. They ought to have shown what each island looked like from the side, through a brass telescope.

He knew there would be other things in store, of course—things not marked on charts—tide rips, whales, and waterspouts—life-threatening dangers. But that was all right. Exploration should be the province of heroes. Peter fingered the white tie around his throat and closed his eyes, which were sore from map-reading. Spots of colour expanded inside his lids, into strange views and vistas: wide green lawns, rowers on a sunlit river, a cream-coloured building like a palace, with tall, narrow stained-glass windows . . . There were no such places in Neverland—none that he had ever seen, at least. Wonderful, then, that there were these pictures in his head!

'*Sail ho!*'

Peter flung down his quill pen and red ink splattered the Sea of a Thousand Islands. He ran up on deck.

'*Sail ho!*' called Curly again from the crow's nest.

'Hardly *sails*, dear,' said Slightly. 'It's a steamer.'

Through Hook's brass telescope Peter sighted a steam-cutter as steel-grey as a knight in armour. Caked in rust like dried blood, it chugged and throbbed and clanked towards them under an awning of dirty smoke from its black smokestack. A jawful of teeth had been painted on to its bow so that it appeared to chew its way through the water. Wendy signalled it with semaphore:

'F-R-I-E-N-D O-R F-O-E?'

The Boys watched with admiration Wendy's outstretched arms moving round like the hands of a clock. Unfortunately the crew of the steamship could none of them read semaphore. They came on, full speed ahead. It was not much of a full-speed, but since the SS *Shark* was on course to ram the *Jolly Peter* amidships, there was no time to lose. No time to load the cannon with gunpowder (or flour). No time to search the ship for muskets.

'*Jibe to port!*' shouted Peter.

The crew blinked at him. They were very impressed, but they had no idea what it meant: Peter must have found a book of sea-going phrases in Hook's sea chest.

'*Steer that way, you lubbers!*' he yelled.

John spun the ship's wheel. The *Jolly Peter* heeled over.

The ship's bell clanged. Sails flapped and billowed. Ropes twanged taut. The puppy slid clear across the deck. The prow of the *Jolly Peter* swung round until she was pointing almost the same way as the *Shark*. Instead of being sliced in two by sheet steel, perhaps they could dodge out of her path or outrun her.

It was a vain hope. The sails emptied of wind; the *Jolly Peter* wallowed and rolled. On and on came the SS *Shark*, so close now that the children could see the pirate flag at the masthead and the crew getting ready to board. They made an unnerving sight, because these pirates, though no more than waist high, were wearing full warpaint and were armed with hatchets, bows and arrows, and bowie knives.

'Starkey's Redskins!' said Peter under his breath.

The steel bow with its painted arc of teeth did not slice open the hull of the *Jolly Peter*. It struck her in the aft quarter, shattering the casement windows of Peter's stateroom and jolting the ship from stem to stern. Powerless to resist, the big brig was pushed through the water ahead of the steam-cutter like a pram being pushed along by a nursemaid. The captain of the steam-cutter was carried for'ard from the bridge, borne aloft on a swivelling leather captain's chair carried by four child warriors. It was none other than Starkey: first mate to Captain Jas. Hook in the long-lost days before Pan's great victory over Hook and his scurvy crew!

'Now what do you say, boys?' Starkey asked, his triumphant features creasing up like old leather. 'Introduce yourselves to the nice people.'

They were not all boys, by any means. Half were girls, with long silken hair and cleaner buckskin tunics. But they were all armed. Drawing back their bowstrings to full stretch, they bowed (or curtsied), blinked their large dark eyes at the crew of the *Jolly Peter* and shouted, 'Hello. Thank you very much. How do you do. Delighted I'm sure. Kindly shed your loot in our direction then lie face down on the deck or, sadly, we will have to slit your gizzards and feed you to the fishes. Deep regrets. Please do not ask for mercy as refusal can give offence. Thank you very much. Nice weather we are having.'

Captain Starkey nodded approvingly and spun round once in his chair. 'Very good, buckos, but you forgot about the scalping. You must always mention the scalping.' Suddenly he seemed to recognize the ship for what it was. Then his eye fell on Peter—or rather Peter's coat—and a lifetime's sunburn could not hide how his face drained of colour.

Meanwhile, the steamship shoved the *Jolly Peter* through the water like a wheelbarrow. They could see now that the name daubed on to the prow of the steam cutter was not 'SS *Shark*' at all, but 'SS *Starkey*'. The wooden hull creaked and groaned. Cannonballs fell from their monkey-racks and rolled down the deck, making both crew and Puppy jump out of their way. Peter's cheeks burned with humiliation.

'Call yourself a captain now, do you, Starkey!' he jeered. 'You were never more than a mop for swabbing Jas. Hook's decks!' One or two of the Explorers had got down on their faces. Now they stood up again, as Peter laughed in the face of his attacker. 'I heard you were captured by the Redskins, Starkey! After we routed you in the Great Battle? I heard you were put to *looking after their papooses*! Terrible fate for a man who calls himself a pirate!' Peter loaded the words with contempt, as he would have loaded a musket.

Captain Starkey spun round twice in his chair. The colour was back in his cheeks. 'Swipe me naked! If it ain't the cock-a-doodle! For a moment I thunk it was . . . Well, ain't revenge sweet, eh? Terrible fate? Yeah! Fate worse than death, I thunk at the time. Forced to look after a bunch of babbies and sprogs? A shame and come-down for a man of my calling! But I made the best of it, see? Turned it to my advantage. See what a job I done on 'em, my little squaws an' braves? You won't find better manners in the King of England's parlour. An' I trained them up in a trade, too, which is more'n you can say for most schoolmasters. Learned 'em everything I knowed. Turned 'em into pirates, every Jack-and-Jill of 'em. Got some real talent in there, I can tell you! Pride of me heart, these little throat-slitters are! Pride of me heart. What's your cargo, cock-a-doodle? Cos it's mine now!'

When Peter refused to answer, Starkey ordered a dozen of his little throat-slitters to board the *Jolly Peter* and hunt for loot. 'And bring me my old kitbag from the fo'c'sle!' he told them. 'The one with me name writ big on it.' When the League bravely drew out their wooden swords to defend the ship, Starkey laughed so much that he nearly toppled out of his chair. 'What? Wouldn't your mummies let you play with real blades?' Even Peter, who always carried a real dagger in his belt, could not defy the twenty arrowheads pointing at his brow.

The warpainted pirates jumped nimbly aboard where the bow of the *Starkey* was wedged in the splintered stern of the *Jolly Peter*. Finding nothing but cobwebs and ship's biscuits in the hold, they rounded up the Darlings and bundled them into the smelly old pirate kitbags from the fo'c'sle, and pulled the cords up tight round their necks: 'I can get me a good price for slaves!' Starkey cackled gloatingly. The warriors were very polite and their small hands were soft and well washed. But they stole John's umbrella and penknife and, as they worked, they discussed whether Puppy was best cooked with ginger, squid, or piri-piri sauce. None of them attempted to lay hands on Peter Pan, who stood defiantly gripping the hilt of his dagger. But they worked round him, ignoring his blood-curdling curses and his promise to 'make Starkey pay'.

All this while, the steam-cutter puffed and chugged and juddered along, pushing the *Jolly Peter* ahead of it like a tea trolley in a Lyons corner house. From the noises it was making, it seemed the brig might die of shame at any minute, burst apart and plunge to the bottom of the sea. After Curly was dragged down from the crow's nest and stuffed into a kitbag, there was no one keeping a lookout for reefs or whirlpools. Without his charts in front of him, Peter had no way of knowing what lay in their path. At any moment they might run aground—or reach the horizon and plunge off the edge of the world! The one thought that comforted him was that the *Jolly Peter* would take the SS *Starkey* with her, down to destruction.

'Turn out your pockets!' Starkey told Peter.

(And put Hook's treasure map into the greedy paws of a common pirate?) 'Never!'

'Turn out your pockets, cock-a-doodle, or I'll have my throat-slitters shoot you full of arrows, and take a look myself, after.'

Wendy saw the boy in the jay feathers and scarlet frock-coat glance towards the ship's rail. She knew at once that he meant to leap to his death sooner than give up the treasure map to Starkey. 'Don't do it, Peter!' she cried.

Starkey laid a fatherly hand on the shoulder of one young squaw, whose bowstring was pulled taut. 'On my word, bucko . . . shoot him in the thigh,' he said, and the squaw took careful aim. 'Let's see what an arrow can do to puncture his pride!'

Now, if Peter *had* had his charts in front of him just then, he would have seen that the Sea of a Thousand Islands had lately gained an extra sprinkling. Five small islands had appeared to port and, most unusually for islands, seemed to be *gaining* on them. What is more, they rose and fell on the swell, riding the waves, travelling against the current. When Starkey saw them too, the sight held him spellbound. The dreaded order 'Shoot' perched unspoken on his lip as he watched the flotilla of little islands sashay closer and closer.

At that very moment, the ancient engines of the steam-cutter, struggling to push the *Jolly Peter* along, overstrained themselves and blew. The funnel coughed up black smuts, then stopped smoking. The sickening forward surge slowed, and both ships were left wallowing. The five islands overtook, nestling closer. They were woolly with trees, alfalfa, and pampas grass, and were apparently hitched to one another by lengths of fraying rope. Did they have inhabitants, these bobbing patches of dry land?

Oh yes.

Grappling irons came over the ship's rail like gigantic claws. After that came . . . well . . . gigantic claws. The Redskins saw the tigers first. The panthers were quicker aboard, but their pelts were so black that they were almost invisible. The bears were slow moving but just as unstoppable, flopping big furry bellies over the rail before flumping on to the deck like sacks of brown sugar. The baboons flew through the rigging, hand-over-fist-over-tail. The palmerions' hooves made a hollow din on the deck-planks.

No doubt Starkey's sprogs were, in the normal course of things, wonderful at archery and throat-slitting. But faced with packs of panthers and a pride of lions, with boarding parties of monkeys and a broadside of bears, their soft little hands shook and the bowstrings slid from between their sweaty fingers. They fled below decks. The search party aboard the *Jolly Peter* leapt back on to the bow of the SS *Starkey*, spilling their captain-nursemaid out of his swivel chair and into the paint-locker. They tried to push off, but the bow of the steam-cutter had wedged itself too deep.

Five islands gently bumped rubber-tree fenders against the *Jolly Peter*. Exotic breeds of animal spilled aboard from four of the five. The fifth island delivered up only one breed of animal. One solitary, two-legged creature.

'Difficulties, sir? What good fortune that I should have been passing,' said the Great Ravello.

CHAPTER NINE
Fair Shares

Peter Pan drew his dagger and cut the cords of seven kitbags. The League of Pan wriggled free. Their first thought was to get as far away as possible from the wild animals roaming the ship, roaring and pouncing and dripping dribble on the deck.

'Oh please!' said Ravello. 'Don't mind my nippers and snappers. They know their place, and they rarely eat between meals.' He cracked his circus-master's whip. The beasts flinched, broke off from what they were doing, leapt over the rail, and swam back to their various floating islands. Except for the bears. They boarded the SS *Starkey* and sat themselves down around the open hatch of the fo'c'sle, dipping huge paws through it as if trying to catch fish through an ice-hole. The little Redskins inside could be heard screaming and whimpering and calling for their mothers. Peter Pan kept tight hold of his dagger.

'Thank you, Mr Ravello!' said Wendy. 'You saved us!'

'Pleasure, ma'am,' said Ravello, bowing. There were scorch marks on his vast garment now, and a smell about him of charred wool. 'I was very much hoping our paths would cross again.'

Peter—tiny alongside the circus-master—flinched. 'Why?'

'There was a fire in the Neverwood—you must have seen something of it as you sailed away. Yes?' (The Twins put their hands over their mouths in guilty horror: was Ravello about to make them pay for burning down his circus? Had he come after them with thoughts of revenge or punishment?) 'My livelihood was utterly destroyed by that fire. Everything gone. Tent, cages, staff . . . Thus I find myself without a profession—without the means of earning a crust.' (The Twins mewed with panic and bitter regret and tried to slide under the tarpaulin of a gig-boat and hide. The Great Ravello intercepted them, a raggedy sleeve encircling each boy, a firm tug pulling their heads close against his body.) 'So. I seek employment. One must work one's passage on the voyage through Life, you do agree?'

'Work's for grown-ups!' said Peter, who didn't.

Ravello waved a ragged sleeve-end and let it drop. 'Ah yes. Of course. I was forgetting. You people here have made Childhood your profession. Sadly I have rather *missed the boat*, in terms of being a little boy. *Ergo*, I must follow some other line of work.' Within the woolly shadow of the hooded cardigan, Ravello's pale brown eyes closed for a moment. 'So I hope—dare I hope?—that I may be allowed to serve, in some humble way, the marvellous Peter Pan.'

Peter was genuinely startled. 'Me?'

Ravello bowed, sweeping the tips of Peter's boots with the ravellings of his cuff. 'Your butler, perhaps! Your valet? Your serving man? I ask no pay, sir! Only my keep, sir! The honour of serving you would be payment enough. Simply to be allowed to be of use, sir! Say you can forgive my sin of growing big, sir!' The shoulders folded forward, the head dipped. A dead sheep would have looked arrogant in comparison with the Great Ravello, as he sank to one knee in front of Peter Pan. 'Let me serve you in any way I can!'

For a moment, Pan could not think what to say. 'What would I call you? Great or Mister?' he asked awkwardly.

'No such formality, sir,' said the Ravelling Man. 'And how should I qualify for the title Great while standing beside yourself? My mother named me . . .' It took him a moment to recall his first name: perhaps he had not used it in a long time. 'My mother gave me the name Crichton, but like most things a mother gives, it is not worth the having. Ravello will do admirably, sir.'

'Good,' said Pan. 'But we are going exploring, you know. I must warn you: it may get dangerous. Courage is everything.'

'You stole the very words from my heart!' said the Ravelling Man, with such intensity that the mercury in the ship's barometer plummeted. 'Courage is indeed *everything*.'

Just then, Starkey wriggled his way out of the paint-locker and peeped nervously over the rail. Seeing him, Peter Pan called sharply: 'What's your cargo, Starkey? Cos it's mine, now!'

The pirate snorted defiantly. 'Shan't tell! Shan't won't!' But as Peter stepped towards him, dagger drawn, the coward fluttered his tattooed fingers in front of his chest and confessed, 'Silverskins, that's what! Don't kill me, Pan! Silverskins!'

Silverskins. A sleek, glittering word. A word with romance to it. Peter nodded solemnly and tilted his head just a little towards Wendy. Wendy tilted her head towards John, John whispered behind his hand to Slightly, '*What's a silverskin?*'

Slightly thought it might be the pelt of an ermine; John thought the peel from a silver nutmeg. Wendy thought of barracuda, silverest fish in the sea. The Twins believed it was a pirate term for a piece of money; Tootles that it was a moonbeam reaped with a sickle. Curly thought fairy slaves.

'You are *indeed* rich, sir,' said Ravello, his eyes wrinkling with joy. 'Silverskins, eh?' So no one confessed that they did not really know, because they did not want to look foolish in front of a grown-up, especially a butler. 'The question is, sir; how will you *share the spoil?* Traditionally (I believe) the captain takes half and divides the rest among his crew.'

That is how it started: the Silverskin War, the Feud of Fair Shares. Before Ravello came along, they would have shared out everything equally. That was how the League of Pan worked: even-stevens. But now Ravello had told them how these things were done.

So now Peter wanted half.

Tootles said that, as a Princess, she should have half too.

Wendy pointed out that, if they were going to start comparing, she was the oldest and she should have half, as well.

Ravello said: 'Of course, another way of sharing out the takings is according to rank.' At which point, the First Sea Lord said that he ought to have twice as much as the Other Sea Lord, and the Mastmaster sneered at the Deckmaster and one got kicked in the ankles. The puppy bit the Best Mate.

Fireflyer said that he was going next door to count the silverskins.

John said they should toss for it: when the coin came down heads and he said 'Heads!', he claimed that he had won the whole lot.

Tootles said that the Twins only counted as one member of crew because they did not have separate names. They would have to share their share.

The Twins said that Tootles could go and boil her head.

Curly said that, strictly speaking, Peter was not the captain of the *Jolly Peter*: he had just helped himself to the title and the captain's quarters.

Peter retorted that if they threw Curly overboard that would mean more silverskins for everybody.

In short, things were said that should never have been put into words—terrible things. Wendy told Peter that he was a selfish baby and had not saved the ship at all. Peter told Wendy that girls did not count as crew, because they were good for nothing. Tootles tried to punch Peter on the nose for that, but missed. Peter grew pompous, then, and said, 'I alone shall decide how the silverskins are divided up!'

Slightly said Peter was so stupid he would not know how to divide a ship's biscuit between two rats.

Within minutes no one was speaking to anyone else. They were slumped in different corners of the ship, raging and sulking and feeling badly done by. John, aiming for

Peter, rolled a cannonball along the deck but it ran over Slightly's hand, which really hurt. Curly refused to go back into the crow's nest to keep watch, because he said they would cheat him out of his fair share as soon as his back was turned. Peter said that, in that case, Curly would be hanged from the yardarm as a mutineer. Worse and worse the insults grew. Ravello was asked to act as referee. But he purred, in his softly cat-like way, that it was 'not his place', adding, with a touch of amusement, that they could always give the loot back to Starkey.

Pan, choking with rage, tugged at the white school tie uncomfortably tight across the throbbing veins in his neck. He called Ravello a fool. He called the League a 'mutinous coterie' and a 'pack of blaggards'—'filchers' and 'pinchers' and 'snappers-up'; 'scurvy dogfish' and 'the scum of the sea'. He said he would strand Tootles and Curly on the next rock, or feed them to the sharks. In fact such a stream of abuse poured out of him that he had to shut his eyes for fear they popped. And when he opened them again, everyone was staring at him. Where had it come from, that outburst? Who had loaded him with such a fusillade of words?

That was when Starkey tried to make his getaway down the anchor chain.

Ravello brought him back—hoiked him back aboard by the scruff of his shirt collar. (Plainly the hands hidden by the dangling sleeves had a grip of steel.)

'Break open your hatches and deliver up your booty!' Peter roared in Starkey's face.

After years spent teaching manners to Redskin sprogs, Starkey said it without thinking: 'Now now, son. What's the little word that gets things done?'

Again that infernal question! Peter searched his head for the magic little word. But he found only cases and cases more of bad-temper. *I don't know! Is it "Flogging"? Or "Plank"? Or "Maroon"?*

Starkey was so scared that he broke open his cargo hold with his bare hands. Out popped Fireflyer (who had squirmed his way in easily enough but had much more trouble getting out). The fairy was so crammed with food that he landed at Peter's feet with a thud like a cricket ball.

'Well, my trusty little spy? What *are* silverskins?'

The fairy burped. *'Onions!'* he said. *'Spring onions!'*

'Onions?!'

Fireflyer burped again. *'There were seven thousand two hundred and eighty-four. I counted,'* he said proudly, *'when I ate 'em.'*

'Stow that fairy belowdecks!' said Pan. 'He has eaten our prize of war!' And his lips curled back from his milk-white teeth in a snarl that would have shamed a shark.

CHAPTER TEN

Lodestone Rock

The Ravelling Man ate only eggs. He ate them raw, out of the shell or, more often, swallowed them down whole. Among the creatures of the floating islands were lizards, snakes, and turtles who laid soft, rubbery eggs, and Ravello always had some about his person, hidden away in the woollen linings of his woollen pockets. Their presence, either in his clothing or on his breath, gave the man his distinctive smell.

He made himself wonderfully useful around the ship, cooking meals, reading the weather, boxing the compass, polishing the brass. He made the Redskins sew their blankets into warm coats for the League. He knew card games and how to tie knots, and the blood-thirstiest pirate stories you ever heard. He took the clapper out of the ship's bell so that it would not disturb them when it rang the night watches (which it still did of its own accord). And at siesta-time, he rocked them to sleep in their hammocks. Ravello himself seemed never to sleep at all, night or day.

To Peter Pan he was most attentive of all, polishing his boots, dusting his cabin—even combing the boy's hair, so that every day it grew slightly longer, slightly darker. It was fun—no doubt about it—to say, 'Fetch me this, Ravello! Do me that, Ravello, and be quick about it!'

The altogether excellent Ravello offered to cut the SS *Starkey* adrift, but it was Peter's first battle prize and he wanted to keep it. So even when the steamer came unwedged, they towed it behind them at the end of a steel chain, while Captain Starkey and his crew were shut up in the fo'c'sle with bears guarding them. The floating islands bobbed in and out of the sea mist, sometimes visible, sometimes quite forgotten.

'What will you do with the Foe, Peter?' asked Wendy. 'Because if you are not going to cut them adrift, I really ought to make them some tea.'

'We'll sell them for slaves or spit-roast them for supper!' Nobody believed him, but he sounded wonderfully decisive. Anyway, he cut such a dash in the tricorn hat and thigh-length boots he had found in the bottom of Hook's sea-trunk: it seemed only right that he should talk like a pirate as well as look like one.

He did take off the scarlet coat for a time. For instance, he took it off to dive overboard where he fought duels with the swordfish, and won their swords from them, so that his Company would never again be caught without weapons. He wrested bones from the mouths of dogfish, too, to feed Puppy. Happily, his bad temper seemed to wash off in the sea.

With all the silverskins eaten, there was no point in them quarrelling any more. The unkind things said could not be rubbed out, but they folded up very small and could be slid away into pockets.

Peter unrolled the treasure map, for everyone to see, and they all gathered round to study the map of Neverland. Inland from the Far Shore and the Purple Moor, the Maze of Regrets, the Elephants' Graveyard, the Thirsty Desert . . . a vast blank was labelled 'UNKNOWN TERRITORY'. At its heart lay Neverpeak, with cartoon clouds around its summit, but inside the Unknown Territory, all tracks and pathways and streams petered out. Landmarks were not listed. Nothing.

'We shall map it as we go!' said Peter.

'And find the source of the Nevva River!'

'Discover new animals!'

'Take rock samples!'

'You might also care to name mountains and lakes, sir,' suggested Ravello, setting down the afternoon tea.

The Explorers were so enchanted with this idea that they instantly began to do it, even before the landmarks had been discovered.

'Bags I the first mountain!'

'The John Darling Falls!'

'Slightly Sound!'

'Twin Peaks!'

'With respect, sir,' purred Ravello, holding up the scarlet coat for Peter to slip his wet arms back inside, 'the area is wrongly marked "Unknown". This Captain Hawk of whom I have heard you speak . . .'

'Hook,' said Peter. 'Jas. Hook.'

'Forgive me. This Captain Hook must have *been* there to deposit his treasure chest. Should it not be "Hook's Territory"?'

'*Peter Pan's!*' cried the One-and-Only Child, circling the whole of Neverland with his raven-quill pen. '*It's MINE! And so is the treasure!*' Red ink spattered Slightly's evening shirt.

There was an awkward silence. '*Ours.* I think the Captain meant to say "*ours*",' said Wendy. 'Didn't you, Peter?'

Peter tugged at the white tie round his neck and coughed. There were bright spots of colour on his cheeks. 'Pour me a tot of Indian courage,' he commanded. 'The smoke from Starkey's filthy pirate barge has turned my stomach.'

'What's the little word that gets things done?' said Tootles without thinking. But Peter glared so fiercely—'*Semolina! Rhubarb! Tapioca! Who cares what the little word is?!*'—that she immediately trotted off to brew a pot of tea.

The tea was never poured. Just as Tootles filled the pot, the *Jolly Peter* pitched and yawed and began to swing about. The steam-cutter had begun dragging her through the water, even though there was no one on her bridge, no fire in her boilers, no smoke in her smokestacks!

In fact the SS *Starkey* was being dragged through the water too—not by another ship but by some invisible power that had gripped her keel. She overtook the *Jolly Peter* and wallowed northward, back-to-front, dragging the brig behind her, her sails turned inside out. The children could only cling on to the fixtures and fittings, wildly guessing:

'It's the mermaids!'

'It's a whale!'

'It's fairy mischief!'

The Ravelling Man ran nimbly down the ladders on his heels, and shouldered his way into Pan's stateroom, to the chart desk. The dirty wool cuffs scrawled circular stains on the vellum as he scoured it for information. Then they banged down on a shaded patch marked 'DANGER AREA'.

'Lodestone Rock!' he said. 'It hauls her in!'

'Magic?' said Slightly.

'Magnetism,' said Ravello.

Soon they could even see it through the brass telescope—Lodestone Rock, a ferrous pinnacle of red rock like a church steeple. Faster and faster the cutter's iron hull sped towards it like a moth towards a flame. The chain between the two ships was stretched so taut that there was no unhitching it.

'*Cub-bages, hie!*' It was a circus-master's voice again, loud and sharp with authority. The bears went over the side. The Redskins swarmed on deck weeping and shrieking and struggling into cork life-jackets. No need for a telescope now. Lodestone Rock loomed up huge in their path, sea foam boiling all around. Their hulls scraped over rock so sharp that it stripped off all the barnacles. The League of Pan clung tightly to the ship's rails—except for Curly who was catapulted out of the crow's nest and into the ocean.

'Throw out the log-line!' shouted Peter Pan, and they stared at him blankly, all except for Ravello who threw down a knotted rope to Curly who was drowning in the churning wake. Curly grabbed hold and was towed along, scuffing the toecaps of his shoes on the razor-sharp rocks beneath him.

The SS *Starkey* struck with the noise of a brass band falling off a tram. The brig, being dragged along behind it, was caught by the swirl of currents around the rock and tossed about so violently that the metal towline snapped like a Christmas paper-chain.

'Now we'll float free!' John asserted. 'The *Jolly Peter* is wooden! Only metal is magnetic!' The *Jolly Peter* was indeed wooden: so what power could the magnetic Lodestone Rock possibly hold over it?

They found out soon enough.

The iron nails holding every rib to the keel, every plank to every rib, every spar to the mast were pulled out by the force of magnetism. Like wasp-stings sucked out of skin, every nail and cleat came out of the timberwork, and the elegant wooden brig began to disintegrate around them.

'*She is gone!*' cried Ravello, falling to his knees, stricken by either fear or grief.

'*Fly!*' cried Peter. John snatched up Fireflyer's top hat, containing its dandruff of fairy dust. The League of Pan plunged in their hands. But in order for it to work, they still had to think happy thoughts, and it was hard to think happy thoughts as the masts tumbled—one! two!—and the hull peeled itself off like an orange.

'*Think of treasure!*' cried Peter. And somehow they all

fastened their minds on Neverpeak and, one by one, rose clumsily into the air.

Peter, of course, arced and swooped with the ease of a summer swallow. He skimmed the wave-tips, to where Curly was floundering in the sea and, grinding a handful of fairy dust into the wet, curly hair, hauled him up from the water by the collar of his rugby shirt. Curly (and the puppy nestled in his pocket) were so happy not to be drowning any more that they quickly gained height and joined the others in the sky over Lodestone Rock.

Below them, the *Jolly Peter* foundered, leaving only a pattern of planks floating on the water. The tall figure of Ravello, balancing on the wreckage, nimbly leapt from driftwood to flotsam, from barrel to spar. Finally he flung himself across a sea chest that came bobbing up to the surface. With white water churning, and the spray coming off the Lodestone Rock, his wool-clad form was soon soaked sodden—a hank of ancient seaweed caught on the lid of the rolling, pitching trunk. Ravello, being a full-grown man (or a very tall cardigan), could not, of course, fly.

A sudden sob broke from Wendy as someone else sprang to mind. Fireflyer, locked up for his greedy wolfing of spring onions, had gone down with the ship!

Chapter Eleven

Grief Reef and the Maze of Witches

Fireflyer bobbed up again like a ship's buoy, his orange hair brighter than the iron-red Lodestone. His little belly was still bulgy with spring onions and his fingers were spiky with cold. You or I would be bluer for being doused in a cold sea, but Fireflyer, after Peter lifted him up, was rather washed-out, like a sock that has been through the laundry too many times. His temper was just as hot, though, and his fairy dust re-dried on him like a crisp candy coat. He flew in fizzing fits and starts and zigzags, until Peter said, 'Stop showing off, fairy, or I'll huff you!'

Sun and moon were both in the sky, with a serving of early stars and a side salad of clouds. Vital to find dry land! But which way to fly? The compass in Neverland has as many points as a frightened hedgehog.

'Do you still have the map, Cap'n?' asked John.

Peter brandished the vellum scroll, but when he tried to open it in mid-air, the wind almost snatched it out of his hands. So they simply flew and, as anxious thoughts took the place of happy ones, sank lower and lower and lower in the air. Spindrift off the wave-tops began to wet their faces, to wash off their fairy dust. Just when things were looking black for the Company of Explorers, they sighted land.

A long, rocky promontory pointed out to sea like a witch's finger, ending in a clutter of rocks and white-water reefs. There were sea-pinks growing in every crevice, and cormorants rose squawking into the air as the Explorers came fluttering down. Oddly, the waterline was strewn with the rusty remains of several hundred prams and baby carriages. Moored up like a rowing boat, on the far side of the headland, was an antique sea chest with the letters **J. H.** on the lid. Oh, and five small islands bobbed at anchor further off shore.

A tall figure stood on the reef, silhouetted against the

sky. A halo of snaky threads coiled all about it, wriggling in the wind; it might have been the Gorgon Medusa waiting to turn someone to stone with a glance. But it was not.

'Welcome to Grief Reef, sir,' said the figure.

Peter was again struggling with the map in the blustery wind. 'Hold this chart flat for me, Ravello,' he said, calm as can be—just as if he had known all along that his valet would be there ahead of him. And Ravello hurried to oblige, cracking the vellum open with a flick of one hand.

It was Ravello who explained about the prams: 'These mildewed and rusting hulks you see before you are all that remain of a hundred sad stories. These are the perambulators and baby carriages once pushed up and down parks and lanes and city streets by nursery maids in charge of baby boys. These are the prams those nursemaids parked up under shady trees while they dozed; or left unattended while they nipped into the post office to buy a stamp; or to flirt with their sweethearts. These are the prams that got out of control because the brake was left off, and ran away down steep hills. In short, these are the prams that boys tumbled out of, never to be seen again. These are the prams that turned baby boys into Lost Boys, and started them on their long journey to Neverland.'

'How do you know all this?' asked Wendy.

The butler gave a stringy shrug. 'I am a travelling man,

miss. Travelling men get around. They hear things. Rumours. Histories. Shall I go on?

'These are the prams the nursemaids frantically searched, when they realized the boys were gone—flinging out bedding and toys and rattles and bootees, gasping and oh!-ing and oh-no!-ing. These empty prams are all the wretches were left with, after angry parents sacked them and sent them away without a reference or a forgiving word.

'These are the prams that the nursemaids rebuilt into little boats, and rowed out to sea, determined to search the world until they found those babies. Hearing tell that Lost Boys were sent to Neverland, they jibed and pitched their way across five oceans, and finally came to grief on Grief Reef.'

At the end of the account, a single question was left hanging in the air, unspoken. Five Lost Boys felt an aching need to ask it, but none of them dared. Wendy spoke it for them. 'And were any Lost Boys ever *found* by these questing nursemaids, Mr Ravello?'

'We must hope not, miss! Indeed we must! For imagine the sour rage in the hearts of those women! Sacked! Turned out-of-doors, without hope of another post! Quite ruined! And for what? For the small error of losing a child. No, no! These ladies did not come looking to *rescue* the boys they had lost. What? They blamed all their woes and sufferings on the babes. All sweetness of nature had been washed out of them by the salt sea. They were half mad from drinking sea water . . . and they were . . . they *are* . . . bent on *revenge*.'

The Lost Boys gulped and turned pale. Peter gave a carefree flick of the hands. 'But they were grown-up, weren't they? So they couldn't get into Neverland, could they?' And everybody felt so much better that they decided to overlook all the grown-up pirates, Redskins, and circus-masters known to inhabit Neverland.

Clambering along the narrow headland, slipping on slimy seaweed and frightening off a pair of seals, the Company of Explorers headed inland for the bruised and purple moors swelling into view. In the very far distance they could see the tiny outline of Neverpeak, goal of their journey. The resourceful Ravello, since arriving at the Reef astride the sea chest, had not wasted his time. While waiting for the children to arrive, he had taken the wheels off a couple of perambulators and fastened them to the trunk, so that now he could haul it bumping and bouncing along behind him. He applied to it for useful items—matches, a pack of cards, tea, pen and ink, and pieces of string. Though the floating islands were left far behind in the bay, along with the animals of the Circus Ravello, he never seemed to run short of the rubbery eggs he ate night and morning.

The children dined, as ever, on food conjured up out of Peter's imagination (although Ravello did bring out a tarnished silver cellar of salt to sprinkle over their dinners).

Surprisingly, Peter's thoughts seemed to have turned to seafood, so that they ate imaginary lobster and turbot, jellied eels and crabmeat paste. (Tootles even broke out in an imaginary rash because she was allergic to whelks.)

The soft squelching ground of the gentle purple moor became drier with every mile they walked. Instead of moss and heather, soon there was nothing but dry dust studded with bristly cactus plants and strung with tripwires of briar and bramble. It was impossible to sit down for a rest, let alone stretch out on the ground and sleep: it would have been like sleeping in a box of needles and drawing pins. They took it in turns to ride on the curved lid of the sea chest.

Caught on the thorns, and dangling from every briar, were rags of cloth—navy serge or striped cotton, faded organdie or the white lace from the hem of a petticoat. Soon enough, the Explorers discovered why. For they came to The Maze.

A wilderness of rippling sandstone, striped with every shade of blue and grey and sad cypress green, had been hollowed out by wind or rain into a honeycomb maze of corridors and passageways. Open to the sky, it whorled and swirled as far as the eye could see, crossing and inter-crossing, so that a person could wander to and fro and never find anything but another corridor to climb, another flume to slide down. And in among these candystripe cones, archways, and gullies of rock, countless women scurried up and down, calling and calling:

'*Henry!*'

'*George!*'

'*Ignatius!*'

'*Jack!*'

Their anxious hands clutched handkerchiefs or small
toys or corners of blanket. Perhaps, after all, it was not wind
or rain that had carved out the soft rock, but the fretful
tread of these women's button boots and sensible shoes, the
swish of their old-fashioned long skirts, as they wandered
the Maze of . . .

'*Witches!* Watch out!' hissed Peter, and the children all
bobbed down.

'They don't look like witches,' said Tootles doubtfully.
'Where are their pointy hats?'

'Grown-ups in Neverland? What else can they be?'
said Pan.

'His lordship is correct, I fear,' whispered Ravello. 'This
is the Maze of Witches. On no account let them see or
touch you or pour their spells in at your ears. These are the
women I told you of.'

'The nursery maids?'

'Precisely. This is where their travels brought them.
Failure and temper poisoned their spirits and turned them
into witches. That's how they magicked their way into
Neverland. But now if they see a child—any child—they
will catch it and wash it; change its socks and feed it

semolina; make it learn its tables and go to bed when it's still light. Like as not, they will probably even *kiss it.*' The boys squirmed and grimaced, pulled their heads down into their shoulders and shuddered. Almost as an afterthought, Ravello said, 'Then they will roast the child and eat it.'

'It was called something different on the map, I thought,' mused Wendy. 'The Maze of . . . something else.' But Peter (still beaming with pleasure at being called 'his lordship') unrolled the map to check, and assured her that yes, yes, it was: The Maze of Witches. (Please remember, though, that he could not read.)

'*Edgar!*'

'*Edmund!*'

'*Paul!*'

'*Jamie!*' The witches kept up their baleful hunting cry. Betweenwhiles, they could be heard sniffing—quite distinctly sniffing—as if to pick up the scent of their prey.

Worming along on their stomachs, grazing knees and wrists on the gritty sandstone, the Explorers inched forward. Within minutes they were hopelessly lost—no longer knew which way they had come, any more than they knew how to get out. Some gulleys were dead ends. Some grew so narrow that the slenderest shoulders would not fit through. Some twisted and turned and doubled back so often that the children lost all sense of direction. John scraped a J in the rock with his swordfish sword-point, and within the next hour they passed the same mark four times over. The un-oiled pram wheels on the sea chest squeaked, and the contents shifted and rattled as it teetered along behind them. But the witches were making so much noise—

'*Shinji!*'

'*Pierre!*'

'*Ivan!*'

'*Ali!*'

—there was no chance they would hear. From behind and ahead, above and below, to right and left came the cries of the witches hunting for children:

'*Percival!*'

'*Richard!*'

'*Billy!*'

'*Rudyard!*'

The rocks gave off a strange smell, too, that brought with it the ache of tears. It was Slightly who began to cry first, big teardrops dripping on to the backs of his hands as he crawled along. The Maze was swimming with sadness, and the sadness was as catching as influenza.

'*Florizel?*'

Directly into their path pattered one of the witches, skirt hems ragged, dance slippers worn through, but the jewels still sparkling around her neck. A bedraggled ostrich feather drooped over her face and she tugged it aside so as to see them better. 'Is it you, Florry? Is it?'

Peter tried to crawl backwards, but collided with Curly. The witch shouted the name over and over again, so loudly that John put his hands over his ears. Other witches were drawn to the noise:

'*Children? There are children?*'

'*Children!*'

Dozens came jostling to catch a glimpse, ran out of their shoes without noticing it, dropped toys and rattles in their haste. Their banshee wailing echoed to and fro. They reached out their arms and cupped their hands and turned their faces up to the sky, saying, '*Please! Please let it be him!*'

The Explorers leapt to their feet and ran, dodging this way and that, heads down, sliding down gulleys and jumping from ridge to ridge. Towed along by Ravello, the sea chest bounded and bounced high into the air, knocking over witches, knocking drinky cups and feeding-bottles out of their hands. Those same hands grabbed at the butler instead, snatching and catching in his woollen garment as if they would pull him apart:

'*Wilfred?*'

'*Matela?*'

'*François?*'

'*Roald?*'

Blinded by tears, Slightly ran straight into another witch— a woman of such hollow-eyed loveliness that his blood seemed to turn to blues music and his heart to pain. For a moment she held his face between her hands, and they stared at each other.

There was a maze, too, in the green iris of her eyes . . . Then Slightly broke away and ran like the very blazes.

In the pocket of the scarlet frock coat the compass banged against Peter's leg. He pulled it out and (for all it had more points than a frightened hedgehog) worked out which way to run. But there were just too many witches. From high and low, right and left, front and back they closed in:

'*Klaus!*'

'*Johann!*'

'*Ai De!*'

'*Pedro!*'

Slightly stopped running. He rested his back against a ridge of rosy, twilit rock, gulping in air, gulping down fear. Then, as the witches flapped towards him in a shrieking mob, he took out his clarinet and started to play.

The notes sobbed through the Maze. A sad, haunting tune it was—but it might as well have been grapeshot fired from a cannon at point-blank range. The witches stopped in their tracks, hands flying to their hearts. Slightly played—the same tune over and over again. From among the ranks of women, a single Scottish voice supplied the words:

> '*Will ye no come back again?*
> *Will ye no come back again?*
> *Better loved ye canna be.*
> *Will ye no come back again?*'

Grief Reef and the Maze of Witches

I dare say you never cry or haven't ever tried it while playing the clarinet, so I'll tell you: your lips won't hold their shape and your nose drizzles. It was hard to play—never harder. Even so, Slightly managed sixteen verses, while the witches swayed and tossed in front of him, like weeping willow trees, and the words echoed round and around. Like Horatius holding the bridge, like Roland at Roncevalles, Slightly played the clarinet while his friends fled to safety. Only when all the women's eyes were shut in an ecstasy of sorrow, and his fellow Explorers had got clean away, did he pick up his heels and **run!**

The whole Company ran, until the soft, striped sandstone under their feet gave way to grass, and even then they kept on running. They ran until there were trees, and the trees held up their branches in surrender: *Stop!* They ran until their lungs hung inside them like dead bats in a cave. Then, panting and gasping and leaning on their knees and deafened by the thudding of their heartbeats, they waited for Slightly to catch them up.

'You were wonderful!' they greeted him.

'So clever!'

'Marvellous!'

'Is it hard to learn?'

The Company of Explorers gathered round Slightly,

praising and congratulating him. (Fireflyer grew so jealous that he bit Puppy.)

'Very fine indeed,' agreed Ravello, fetching the makings of afternoon tea out of the sea chest. 'You are to be congratulated, young sir, on your musical genius.'

Slightly blushed redder and redder. 'They seemed more sad than angry,' he said (being sensitive to other people's feelings). 'Those ladies: are you sure they wanted to eat us?'

'A few may be vegetarians,' said Ravello quickly, then drew Slightly aside to shake him by the hand. (That is to say, Slightly found his palm filled with crinkled wool.) 'It is entirely thanks to you that we escaped! Such skill, such artistry! A maestro in the making! I suppose that is what you wish to be, is it? When you are grown-up? A musician?'

Slightly's ears were still pink from all the praise. 'Me?' he said, searching for enough of Ravello's face to see if he was teasing. But the pale brown eyes fastened on his were earnest and intense, while the sleeve unravelled and unravelled. Whole hanks of wool filled Slightly's hands.

And all at once he saw a picture in his head, like reflections in a Hall of Mirrors: himself a grown man, a thousand tunes tucked away inside his head like the doves in a magician's top hat; playing the clarinet with never a single wrong note; a host of faces smiling with pleasure as, with pursed lips and closed eyes, he blew music out into the world like so many soap bubbles.

'Oh yes!' said Slightly. 'I would *love* to be one of those when I grow up!'

'Then who can prevent it?' said the Ravelling Man, and his eyes flashed with pure delight before he turned away.

CHAPTER TWELVE
Fare Shares

He never slept. Wendy (who tucked in everybody else at night and listened to their dreams each morning) could not help but notice: the Ravelling Man never slept at all, but sat up all night, darning his tattered garment. He was so adept with needle and wool and he could do it one-handed. Meanwhile, his eyes scanned the darkness and his head tilted this way and that as he listened for . . . for what? Danger? He must be guarding them from danger, but Wendy preferred not to ask what kind.

The Explorers saw any number of wonders in the days that followed. They saw hills that rose and fell, breathingly.

They saw rivers that flowed uphill, flowers that opened their trumpets and sang, trees that snatched birds out of the sky and ate them, pebbles that floated like corks. John trod on a mirage and sank up to his waist, whereas Tootles managed to cross a river using only the fish for stepping-stones. Once, it even rained conkers—and not one tree in sight.

'What happened to summer?' asked Slightly, half remembering sunnier times.

But Pan only shrugged as if he had not noticed. 'I suppose it got lost,' he said.

To pass the time, they discussed what they would find when, finally, they reached Neverpeak and the treasure chest hidden there. The Twins suggested gold doubloons and pieces of eight and nine. But in Neverland, rainbows stand with both feet on the ground, so, when the weather is right, you can easily go to the end of some rainbow and dig up a pot of gold, if that's what takes your fancy. Consequently, there is nothing very marvellous about gold coins (unless they are chocolate inside).

Tootles thought there would be crowns and tiaras, diamond necklaces and golden pocket watches. 'That's the sort of thing Hook would steal from the poor helpless princesses and sultanas who fell into his merciless hands!' she said.

Fireflyer thought sherbet lemons. Puppy was hoping for

mutton chops. Wendy thought bolts of Indian silk, hand-coloured picture books, and Fabergé eggs from Russia.

'Fabergees don't lay eggs,' said Peter with a snort of contempt, though he did not say what treasure *he* expected to find in the chest. Ravello, running the comb slowly through Peter's hair, curling the glossy locks around a pencil, said nothing at all.

'What would you wish for, Mr Ravello?' asked Wendy.

The comb came to a halt. The brows knit in a way that suggested a fearful headache raging behind the valet's eyes. 'I cannot wish, miss,' Ravello said. 'No more than I can dream. To do either, a man needs sleep. And I do not sleep, you see.'

'It all depends what Hook prized most in all the world,' said Slightly who had been riding along in his own private train of thought. 'Cos that's what treasure is, isn't it? The thing you want most of all in the whole world to keep and have for your own?'

At which Fireflyer squeaked: *The eyeballs of his enemies!* and everybody threw things at him. *'What?'* he protested. *'I 'spect pirates eat eyeballs 'stead of sherbet lemons! What's for supper?'*

Ravello brought out the tablecloth and spread it on the ground, with the salt in the middle. They all sat round, cross-legged, and Peter began to imagine them something to eat.

'What's on the menu, Cap'n?' asked John, patting at the creased white linen.

A frown creased Peter's forehead, so that his eyebrows cocked like little angel-wings. 'I forget,' he said. 'I'm not hungry. You can eat mine if you like.'

Everyone reached for the invisible food. There was a faint smell of cauliflower and privet. Curly thought his fingers had brushed a cabbage or a spoon, but nobody could quite lay hands on their portion of food. Slightly, who was having trouble stowing his long legs under him, reached out clumsily and knocked over the salt.

'*By Kraken and Krakatoa!*' bawled Peter Pan jumping to his feet. '*Put stones in that boy's boots and feed him to the fishes!*' The League stared at him, startled. Peter glared back. '*Didn't you see? What are you all, blind? The clumsy swab spilled the salt! Does he mean to bring down bad luck on us all? By all the shanks in me ratline, I've a mind to brand him or strand him here and now!*'

All eyes turned on Slightly, who blushed, righted the salt pot and apologized.

'I didn't know you were superstitious, Peter,' said Wendy, worried by the way the big purple veins were beating in his small white neck.

'I once saw five black cats . . .' Tootles began, but broke off, not able to remember whether black cats brought good luck or bad.

'*One for sorrow, two for joy* . . .' said one Twin.

'That's magpies,' said his brother. 'Or babies.'

The meal lapsed into silence, then broke up, because meals do not last very long when there is nothing to eat. When they set off to walk again, Slightly was sent to the back of the line. Nobody liked to mention that they had had no supper, in case the Leader lost patience with them, too. Ravello shook the offending salt off the tablecloth, folded it up and put it back in the sea chest, first removing Fireflyer, who had fallen asleep in the collar drawer. Puppy wandered off in search of something more filling than nothing at all.

Still quivering, like a cat that has been stepped on, Slightly hung back from the rest. He was glad when Fireflyer came and rode on his shoulder. Fireflyer did not care if Slightly had suddenly grown clumsy; he was devoted to the boy who called him a 'whopping liar' and who could produce musical notes from A to G. *'When you get bigger will you play the rest of the alphabet?'* Fireflyer asked.

'No,' said Slightly. 'You'll have to make do with A to G.'

Fireflyer liked nothing better than to chase the notes that came from Slightly's clarinet—to eat them like chocolates, out of the air. The breves were best—fat and round, with creamy centres. The demi-semi-quavers were fizzy, but it took dozens just to make one mouthful. The sharps were sharp as lemons, and the flats slipped down like slices of cucumber cut very thin. Slightly laughed to see the fairy bite into them, making them pop: it took his mind off the shock of being shouted at by Peter.

'More music! More music!' urged Fireflyer.

'What's the little word?' said Slightly, who knew the importance of good manners.

'Dunno,' said Fireflyer, who did not.

The higher the note, the higher Fireflyer had to fly to pop it. 'What can you see from up there?' Slightly called, as the fairy soared after a top G.

'Oooo. Far as far! Mount Etna and the Po River!' called Fireflyer. *'Higher! Higher!'*

'Little liar!' called Slightly, and played a higher scale. Fireflyer flew up and up and up . . . 'Now what can you see?'

'Ooo. Right over the horizon! Constantinople and Timbuktu! Higher! Higher!'

'Little liar!' said Slightly with a smile, and when he had played the topmost note on the clarinet, put it away and began to whistle instead. 'Now what can you see?'

'Oooo. Right into the past! I see the Aztecs and the Vikings!' called Fireflyer, through a mouthful of crotchets. *'Higher! Higher!'*

'Little liar!' said Slightly and laughed, and whistled again, even more shrilly.

'Belay that whistling, you swab!' Suddenly Peter Pan stood in front of him, cheeks fiery red, eyelids straining wide. *'Do you mean to whistle up Bad Luck?'*

The hairs stood up stiff with terror in the nape of Slightly's neck. 'Sorry, Cap'n,' he whispered.

'Do you not know it's unlucky to whistle on board ship!?'

'But we're not on . . .' whispered Slightly, his words tailing away in the face of Peter's rage.

'Ooo! I see lurkers and pouncers!' fluted Fireflycr high above their heads. *'Underbushy ambushers!'* But no one took any notice, of course, because he was always lying. *'Fairies die if people ignore them!'* he complained.

Peter set two flat hands on Slightly's chest and gave him a push, so that he fell over backwards. 'Walk further off, can't you? Keep your bad luck to yourself!'

The other Explorers looked at one another. Tootles's lip trembled, and her fingers, without realizing, stroked at her top lip. Ravello seemed not to have heard the ruckus, and pressed on, head down, towing the sea chest into a wood. They fell into step behind him, single file, because the path was narrow. Wendy walked just behind Peter, watching the tails of the red coat swash to and fro and his long curly hair bounce prettily on his collar. 'You do not seem quite yourself, Peter,' she said. 'Truly, I hardly recognized you just now.'

'Well,' said Peter, 'this adventuring is so boring! We have not had a single battle since we landed!' But then he coughed, and mopped his brow with Wendy's borrowed handkerchief, and he did not turn to look at her, not even once.

Leafy woods gave way to lifeless pine forests. After sunset, when they sat down to supper, Peter announced that there would be no food for Slightly, because he had whistled, and whistling was unlucky (at which Wendy promptly resolved to give all her supper to Slightly). The rest of the expedition waited, and their mouths watered, and some hoped it would be lemon cake and some that it would be sausages . . .

But the truth was, there was no food for anyone. Nothing appeared on the white tablecloth. Time and time again Peter tried to imagine it there. When apple strudel would not come, he tried for simple fruit and veg. But though the League felt around and beyond their plates, eagerly patting their hands over the tablecloth, they felt no invisible oranges, no celery or carrots or even kale.

'The birds must have eaten it out of my head,' said Peter aghast. 'Or greedy fairies. Or it's that bad luck Slightly brought down on us with his salt-spilling and his whistling.'

Whoever the culprit was, his magical gift was gone, as surely as a book stolen from a library, and the League went to bed hungry—so hungry they could not sleep. The moon looked like a round Dutch cheese and the stars like breadcrumbs. The hum of insects sounded like soup simmering, the plop of rain like the clop of the milkman's horse. Their stomachs gurgled. They were so hungry that they even thought longingly of Ravello's rubbery eggs and wondered if he might be persuaded to share . . .

'There are, of course, ship's biscuits in the sea chest,' said his deep and velvety voice out of the darkness.

Within seconds they were clamouring round the sea chest, searching by the light of glow-worms and fireflies, and trying to remember how to divide three-and-thirty biscuits between eight hungry mouths.

'When we find them we must make them last!' said Wendy, being sensible. 'Nobody must eat their ration all at once.'

They turned out books and sea boots, a sou'wester and a life-jacket, inkwell and pens, charts and compasses. But all they found at the bottom were the wrappers off three packets of biscuits, and a sprinkling of weevils.

'F-I-R-E-F-L-Y-E-R!'

The fairy had eaten every last one.

Hunger menaced then, as surely as a pack of wolves, for Peter's gift was gone, and so were all their rations. When Fireflyer had sneaked into the sea chest and helped himself to the last eatables, he might as well have poisoned the tea or burned their warm clothing. They looked around them at the landscape and it was no longer friendly, no longer opening its coat flaps to share wonders with them. It was just a larder, vast and hostile and EMPTY.

Do you know the worst thing about fairies? They never say sorry. Those same little mouths that are so quick to gobble musical notes, biscuits, buttons, acorns, and spring onions simply cannot get their teeth round the words 'please' or 'sorry'. So when Peter summoned the greedy little creature before him and asked what Fireflyer had to say for himself, the little blue gobbler only shrugged and said, *'I was hungry!'* as if that explained everything.

Peter drew out his sword—'*Oh, Peter, no!*'—and drew a window in the air—a casement complete with glazing bars, sill, and latch. Then he opened it and shooed Fireflyer out, like a summer wasp that has found its way indoors. 'I shut you out, pest, for taking more than your fair share!' The window closed: they all heard the latch click. From beyond it, Fireflyer called, *'Fairies die if you ignore them, you know?'* but they were forbidden to answer. Hunger grumbled in eight small stomachs. They rolled themselves in their blanket coats and slept, in the hope they might dream of food.

In the morning, they woke to find the tablecloth spread on a bed of pine-needles and Peter sitting cross-legged beside it. He had taken off his red coat to use as a cushion. In front of him were ranged eight plates, and he was counting out berries into equal portions. 'One for you. One for him. One for her. Two for the Twins. One for . . .' Seeing them watching, he raised a bunch of glistening red fruit in salute. 'Fare shares!' he said and laughed.

'Where did you . . . ?' Wendy began in astonishment.

'I flew about by moonlight! I followed the owls and I shadowed the bats. Where the bee sneaks, there snuck I. Oh, the cleverness of Pan!' There was still something of the moonlight in his face; a silvery pallor: moon tan.

'I think we may say that His Excellency the Wonderful Boy has saved the day,' said Ravello bowing reverentially and helping Peter back on with his scarlet coat. In their delight, the Twins began to clap, and the rest of the Darlings joined in.

The berries were scarlet and bullet-hard. One might taste of cherries, the next more like tomato or smoked ham. Ravello sprinkled them liberally with salt. To soften the pips, he said. Peter Pan barely remembered to eat his portion, he was so busy revelling in the words 'His Excellency the Wonderful Boy'.

Later, as they passed through a dense dark grove of piny trees, the Wonderful Boy pointed out where he had picked them, high among the upper branches; the Twins ran over to jump and snatch, but they were far too tiny to reach. Wendy could not, nor could Tootles. Not even Curly, come to that. As Peter rose effortlessly off the ground, to pick some more for the journey, the others clenched their fists, bent their knees and tried to muster happy thoughts for all they were worth. A cold, drizzling rain and a shortage of fairy dust made it difficult.

Slightly, eager to make himself useful and to put himself back in Peter's good books, hurried up from the rear, stood on tiptoe, reached up as high as he could, and picked three bunches of scarlet fruit.

'*Carve the name out of that boy and cast him adrift!*' Feet planted wide on a high bough, one hand on his sword, Peter Pan pointed a damning finger at Slightly, speaking the words that every Lost Boy dreads to hear. '*Cull him for a traitor and a turncoat! Send him to Nowhereland! Let no one speak to him ever again!*'

'Oh, Peter!' cried Wendy reaching up a restraining hand, but there was no touching Pan, who perched on the bough like some terrible eagle eyeing its prey. She had to tip her head right back on her neck, and the rain fell into her eyes. 'Oh, Peter! What has he done? He only picked some . . .'

Pan swooped down, terrifying, hawkish. He snatched the swordfish sword from Slightly's belt and broke it across his knee. 'Do you not see? The breaker of oaths! The big long snake-in-the-grass!' He came to rest as he had before, face-to-face with Slightly (except that now his nose was on a level with the top button of Slightly's shirt).

Perhaps it was the doing of that witch, holding Slightly's face between her hands. Perhaps it was because he had entered Neverland by foul means (tunnelling down to the end of his bed). Perhaps it was the fault of Time as it prowled Neverland, turning the summer greenery to red and orange, setting the ship's bell ringing. Or perhaps he really was a traitor. Whatever the cause, Slightly Darling was *growing up*—no denying it. Already he stood head-and-shoulders taller than Peter and could reach the berries no one else could reach from the ground.

Peter drew his sword—'*Oh, please, Cap'n, no!*'—and with the swordpoint drew a portcullis in the air, complete with rope and wheel and cruel iron spikes. Then he raised the portcullis, drove Slightly backwards through it on the end of his sword, and lowered the grille again, shutting him out.

'You all swore not to grow up,' said Peter, daring anyone to object. 'That is the only Rule. And Slightly broke it.'

How could they argue? Again the Explorers fell in one behind another, single file, and resumed their long trek towards Neverpeak. Glancing back over her shoulder to where Slightly stood motionless in the rain, Wendy saw that his evening shirt now barely reached to his knees, and the clarinet in his hand seemed smaller than it had before. Distance helped. The further away they got, the smaller he looked, that pathetic figure on the pathway. You might almost have mistaken him for a little boy lost in the rain.

CHAPTER THIRTEEN
Taking Sides

A haunting, yearning music floated to them on the breeze. First thing every morning and last thing every night, the sound of Slightly's clarinet came to them out of banishment. Nobody had quite expected that. They understood that Slightly had done wrong by growing, and they wanted to shut him out of their minds, as Peter had told them they must. But it is hard to forget someone while they are still within earshot.

The going was getting hard. Pine forests had given way to mere trunks—a landscape of naked sticks as leafless and lifeless as ships' masts on a sandbank. The mapmaker had called this place the Thirsty Desert, but that was patently wrong. For it was not the *desert* which was thirsty at all: it was anybody travelling through it. There were no lakes or rivers to drink from, and what with the salt on their dinners, the Company of Explorers were quite parched. Peter had gone on ahead to scout about for a spring or a brook. Once more Slightly's music drifted to them on the wind.

'Whatever will become of him?' said Wendy.

She was merely thinking aloud, but Ravello looked up from cleaning Pan's boots and answered her.

'He will doubtless become one of the Roarers, miss, and run wild and wayward, and dine on dishes of cold revenge.'

'Yuck,' said a Twin. 'Is that like rice pudding?'

Ravello spat on the leather, for want of boot-polish, and worked up a shine using the tail of his shapeless cardigan. 'Not quite, Master Darling, sir. Did you never hear the saying: "*Revenge is a dish best served cold*"? Of course, the Witches may catch him first.'

'Who are the Roarers?' asked John, fearing for a moment that Slightly might enjoy himself more with them than with the Explorers.

'The Roarers?' Ravello seemed surprised at their ignorance. 'I would have thought His Supreme Highness would have told you about them long ago.' (How Peter would have delighted in 'His Supreme Highness', if he had been there.) 'The Roarers. The Long Boys. The Long, Lost Boys. They are the ones Peter Pan culled for breaking the Rule. For growing up. He turned them out, and now they roam the wild places, living by banditry and mayhem. Cruel through and through.'

'No one is all bad,' said Wendy quickly, knowing Slightly could never do such things.

The valet's voice was not quarrelsome. It remained as gentle and springy as a lamb. 'Why would any sweetness linger, miss? Consider. Neglected and mislaid by their mothers, they are posted away to Neverland, their hearts in their boots. But—oh! the blessed relief!—they find themselves welcomed into the cosiness of den and tree house, into a world of friends and fun. They belong again! Life is perfect! Then one day their wrist-bones poke out below their cuffs; their trousers are too short. And for this sin they lose their place in Paradise. They are banished— put out-of-doors like an empty milk-bottle—despised and rejected—and this time by their *very best friend*.'

The League flinched. There was a sharp drawing in of breath. Put that way, it sounded so . . . unkind.

'They cannot go home, for they are adult, and adults (as you know) cannot fly. So they are trapped in Neverland, but without any of the joy and benefits that should bestow. Their hearts canker, like apples left too long on the tree; Hate and Regret burrow deep as caterpillars. Consider.

Love is learned at our mother's knee,' purred Ravello, 'betrayal when she tires of us and her skirts swish away into the distance. If friends turn their backs too—well! Why not banditry? Why not throat-slitting? Why not a life of crime? Despair kills the heart in a boy.' He held up the boots he was polishing, an arm down each leg, to admire the glossy leather. 'No. I have tamed bears and I have tamed lions, miss. By a mixture of love and fear, I have tamed all breeds of animal. But there is no taming the Roarers. They have nothing left to fear, and wisely they have learned never again to love.' The polished boots stood on the ground in their midst now, as though Pan stood there, but invisibly. The circus-master bowed extravagantly low to these empty boots. 'But! Mr Slightly broke the Golden Rule and Mr Slightly has paid the price. What choice did the Marvellous Boy have? Such is the Law of Pan.'

The sound of Slightly's clarinet swooped over their heads like a summer swallow, and everyone but Ravello ducked their heads, fearful of it tangling in their hair.

Out of that same sky Peter returned, each foot sliding home into its shiny boot like a knife into a sheath. He had news of a waterfall up ahead, and the Company of Explorers, now all parched with thirst, jumped up and hurried on.

It was a waterfall complete in itself: no river flowing up to the brink, no river flowing away—simply a cascade of water cloaking a wall of rock as high as the Nevertree and as smooth as glass. They stood as close as they dared, mouths wide open, letting the icy spray drift into their throats. It was delicious. As white and drifting as smoke, the spray enveloped them, silvering their hair with water droplets. When the sun broke through, and shone on the drifting spray, there were rainbows too. And when, high above their heads, there formed a cloud of flittering, glittering colour, they gasped at the sheer Beauty of it.

Not that Beauty ranks high on a child's wish list. He wouldn't spend his pocket money buying it. He would not scrape the bowl clean if it was served up for dinner. In fact, on most days, Beauty never got a mention or a passing thought. But this particular sight cast a spell of rare wonder over the Explorers, and they stood gazing up at the kaleidoscope of shifting lilac, blue, mauve, and purple. What is it that writer-man said? *Sometimes Beauty boils over and then spirits are abroad.*

One by one, the individual flecks of colour separated and floated down, like rose petals at the end of summer. They brushed the upturned faces; settled on their shoulders. More and more fell: a light snow of flaking colour. Like snow it mesmerized them—a dizzying downward whirl of prettiness. Instead of spray from the waterfall they could feel only the soft touch of a thousand

thousand velvety fragments of loveliness. It piled up in their hair; it filled their ears and pockets; it tugged on their clothing. Tugged?

'Fairies!' cried Tootles delightedly. 'Thousands of fairies!'

Suddenly the snow was a blizzard. Delight was replaced by unease then, just as quickly, by fear. The snowfall of tiny bodies showed no sign of stopping. Soon the children were floundering ankle-deep, knee-deep in drifts of fairies, unable to take one step. Their hands, caked with fairy-glamour, were too heavy to lift. Tootles's yellow plaits were blades of corn encrusted with locusts. The weight bore the children down, dragged them down, pressed them down. Those left standing struggled to stay upright, for those who lost their footing were instantly overwhelmed—buried—under a ton of fairies. But one by one they fell, and one by one they were smothered under a carpet—a mattress—a haystack of fairy ambushers. Pinioned to the ground, they could hear nothing but the click of a million tiny wings, the hiss and buzz of a million vicious little voices.

> *'What side? What side? What side are you?*
> *Are you Red or are you Blue?*
> *Answer now and answer true!*
> *Are you Red or are you Blue?'*

'Did that treacherous little onion-gobbler send you?' grunted Peter Pan. But it was already plain that this was not some practical joke or peevish prank. The Explorers had walked into the middle of a fully-fledged war. The Fairies began to pinch and kick. The Twins (remembering Fireflyer's appetite) thought they were being eaten and started to cry. Again and again the tiny, massed voices vibrated through them, like choirs of bees:

> *'Show your banner: Blue or Red.*
> *Show your flag or lose your head.*
> *Nothing else will rescue you!*
> *Are you Red or are you Blue?'*

Clearly the world of fairies had split in two, and a war was waging between two great armies—the Red faction and the Blues. Wendy racked her brains to think what the quarrel might be about: what the colours might signify. She remembered that girl fairies are white and that boy fairies are lilac and that those too silly to make up their mind are blue. But this could not be a war of the sexes: there were both males and females among the swarm of attackers. It was so unfair: to have to take sides without knowing what each side stood for!

> *'Are you with us, are you not?*
> *Are you cool or are you hot?*

> *Are you Blue or are you Red?*
> *Answer wrong and you are dead.'*

Their captors chanted their rhymes without any excitement. They must have sung them so often that they no longer even noticed what they were saying. That did not make the words any less chilling.

'We are not on any side!' grunted Curly, scarcely able to muster the breath. 'We're like the Swiss!'

'Swiss?' panted John, who was very patriotic. 'We're British!' If Curly had been able to move a foot, he might have kicked John. Anyway, the fairies did not give a fig for neutrality.

> *'Are you friend or are you foe*
> *Say before we let you go—*
> *Let you live, or make you die.*
> *Say what colour flag you fly.'*

Wendy tried to tell them: 'Our flag's the sunflower-and-two-rabbits!' She tried to say, 'We're Explorers! We're not at war with anyone!' But there were fairies in her mouth, and a fairy army stoving in her ribs. Anyway, it seemed that the fairies would ignore any answer but 'Red' or 'Blue'.

And if the children guessed and guessed wrong, it would be the last word they ever spoke.

'Take a side. Take a side.
Tell us how your flag is dyed.
Raise your flag and raise it high.
If you don't, PREPARE TO DIE.'

'How can we raise our flag unless you get off us!' raged Peter. Perhaps the swarm relented, or perhaps the One-and-Only-Boy was so furiously determined that he thrashed his way to the surface. But there he was at last, at the foot of the waterfall, upright despite the canker of fairies swinging on his white necktie. *'We sail under the Skull-and-Crossbones!'* he declared. *'That's our flag!'*

'Peter, *no*! That's not true!' Wendy was so shocked that she too wriggled free.

Her eyes met his, and it seemed for a moment as if the words had surprised Peter as much as her. Luckily, 'skull-and-crossbones' meant nothing to the chanting fairies: they did not know what colour of flag a pirate flew. Less luckily, their patience was at an end.

'Are you Reds or are you Blues?
Do you win or do you lose?
Dead in three unless you choose
Are you Reds or are you Blues? ONE—'

All of a sudden, a halo of light exploded about Peter's

slight form. Then he disappeared utterly from sight. He had stepped backwards through the cascading waterfall. Wendy was both thrilled and appalled—thrilled that their Captain had escaped, appalled that he had left his friends to the mercy of the fairies.

'TWO!'

There was nothing for it. They would have to guess—guess Blue and hope that they were not in the hands of the Reds—or Red and hope that they were not among Blues. Every member of the League of Pan called the colours to mind, and tried to decide. Neither blue nor red seemed good enough to die for.

'RAINBOW!'

Back through the screen of water, out of the noisy spray, came Peter Pan. In his hand flapped one of the rainbows formed by sun and spray. 'Here is our banner! Now judge us by our flag, sprites, and kill us or free us!'

The fairy army was thrown into confusion. They looked at the banner, woven out of spray and sunlight, and saw both blue and red in equal proportions—as well as a host of other colours. The press of tiny bodies lessened as fairy-gravity took hold. (Fairies always fall upwards.) They looked mildly cheated, for Peter had spoiled their fun: armies enjoy killing more than making new friends. They eyed enviously the rainbow banner, too, almost as if they preferred it to either Red or Blue. Then, forming a spinning tornado-funnel of glittering bodies, they whirled away into the sky.

Wendy wanted to call out to them: *Stop! Don't! You never used to fight! What are you thinking of!* But the cloud of lilac and mauve and indigo, of blue and purple and white, tumbled skywards, finally separating like rice at a wedding. Or an exploding shell.

'Them and their stupid flags,' said John, but the littler ones were gazing at their Captain and saluting his marvellous rainbow banner. Peter had mounted it on a pole. Now its spray-and-sunlight fabric furled and unfurled over their heads as he gave the order: 'Fall in, me hearties! Who's for Neverpeak and a chest full of treasure?'

The mountain was so close now that it filled one whole horizon. They could easily see its surplice of snow, its flanks scarred by rockfalls. It was unimaginably high.

Within the hour, they passed the scene of a fairy battle, the ground scattered with ten thousand ragged wings, the cobwebs clogged with fairy dust. Fat, black crows hopped about, glossy and villainous.

'How long have the fairies been fighting each other?' Wendy asked, trying to take care where she trod, holding on to the back of Peter's coat. Peter swished and swashed the rainbow flag this way and that, for the fun of seeing the crows jump up into the sky. 'Peter! What are the Reds and Blues fighting *about*?'

He laughed, and skipped over a pile of fairy catapults made from the wishbones of wrens. 'Well, their favourite colour, of course! Which is best.'

The sea chest, mounted on its springy pram wheels, creaked and rattled as Ravello towed it over the bumpy battlefield. 'Fairies travel,' he observed. 'They pick things up. Souvenirs. Head colds. Ideas. I dare say this War of theirs is some idea they brought home from overseas . . . like black rats bringing the Plague!' Then he smiled at some fleeting thought, and murmured in silken tones, 'Or perhaps the fairies left open the night windows of Neverland. And in came War.'

The Ravelling Man stopped speaking to listen, cocking his hooded head first one way, then another, as he frequently did. He said he was partial to birdsong and was listening for nightingales. But Wendy could hear nothing— not nightingales, not even Slightly's clarinet.

Only the plump crows cawing.

CHAPTER FOURTEEN

No Fun Any More

At the foot of Neverpeak Mountain lay scarlet bogs and swamps, as innocent-looking as parlour carpets, but as deadly deep as graves. The Company had to watch their every step, for straying off the path might sink them in quicksand and leave nothing to show for Pan's Quest but a bubble of marsh gas. Between the swamps grew mangroves and mandrakes, corkscrew-dogwood and dog-tooth corkwood oozing amber gum. There was no food to be had, except for the berries they had picked earlier and brought with them. Ravello counted these out on to the Explorers' plates at mealtime, keeping none back for himself.

The only trouble was, the berries brought on dreams, and the only trouble with dreams is that there is no choosing which ones you get. They arrive like the weather, blown in from north or south, past or future, dark places or light. Dreams float seven-eighths beneath the water.

Tootles dreamed she was a man wearing worsted trousers, a red robe, and a big moustache—which was very confusing.

Wendy dreamed of a little girl called Jane asleep in a moonlit bedroom. The girl dreamed Wendy and Wendy dreamed the girl, and when their sleeping eyes met, the child sat bolt upright and cried, 'Mummy!' It churned up the blood in Wendy's heart like the lees in a bottle of port wine.

The Twins dreamed each other's dreams, which was fine.

John dreamed of his brother Michael and woke up crying.

Curly dreamed of Slightly, who was calling to him, telling him to beware, but the dream unravelled before he could find out why.

But Peter! Peter had a marvellous dream of somewhere he had never been, somewhere aswarm with boys all older than himself, all strangers, playing games he had never played, crowding into buildings he had never seen. He was rowing a skiff over sunlit water, and his legs were not long enough to reach the footboards. He was dressed in white, pitching a ball at three wooden sticks in the ground, and he knew that something vital depended on it. He had to sing a song he did not know, in a language he did not understand.

And he was so HAPPY and so AFRAID and so HOPEFUL, because just around the river's bend, just at the top of the grand stairs, just beyond Agar or Jordan or Luxmoore's Garden or Fellows' Eyot—what were these places and how did he know their names?—he would find the treasure, the whole wonderful . . .

They were woken by the sound of Slightly's clarinet. It was playing the same tune he had played to the witches, back at the Maze:

> *'Better loved ye canna be.*
> *Will ye no come back again?'*

And they shouted for him to go away, but he just went on playing.

They had pitched camp at night, unaware how close they had come to the mountain itself. Now, in the dawn light, it rose above them, higher than high, its head in the clouds and its feet fourteen storeys underground. Neverpeak stretched up and away: granite cliffs and marble precipices, pumice ledges and slaty slopes of scree. It was the shape of a cupcake, steep sides rising to a bumpy mound of white icing. Glaciers had cut helter-skelter grooves, round and around. Lightning had burned it bare. Thunder rolled around its ravines. And Neverpeak was so vast that it turned back the wind, as dry land turns back the sea.

'Oh, Peter!' said Tootles. 'Won't you fly up to the top and fetch back the treasure?'

'Idle, mutinous moll!' shouted Peter, scaring Tootles so much that she ran to Wendy and asked for a hug. 'What are you: Explorers or lily-livered scupper-rats born with your tails in your mouths? Leading you is like dragging anchor! You're a cargo of sour milk! You're a waste of rations, that's what you are!'

'What rations?' asked First Twin, reminded of his hunger. His brother tried to shush him, but it was too late. Pan turned his tirade from Tootles to First Twin and then to every other boy, telling them they were turncoats and whiners, mutineers and fair-weather sailors.

'They are just tired, Peter,' said Wendy gently. 'Tired and hungry. Couldn't we . . .'

'What are you, the fo'c'sle lawyer? So it's you who's been turning them against me, is it? I should have known! Girls! What are they good for but growing into mothers, and everyone knows what *mothers* are!' Wendy gasped. Peter's cheeks flashed fiery red and he wrenched at the flaps of his frock coat, sweating with rage, panicky to be out of it. 'Coat, Ravello!'

Ravello stepped sharply forward, but only to try and persuade him back into the scarlet. 'The air is chill, milord. I beg you to keep its warmth around you.' Peter tugged off the coat and threw it at him.

Round the base of the mountain, huge monkey-puzzle trees, dark and crooked, flattened themselves against vertical cliffs, like cornered villains with their backs to a wall. Big wasp's nests balanced in the crook of every branch. Now Peter leapt away from the Company of Explorers and began to climb the trees—hand-over-hand—showing off with leaps and somersaults, proving how simple it was, even for those with too little fairy dust to fly. The Darlings hesitated, daunted by the monstrous mountain.

Ravello opened the sea chest, folded and put away the frock coat. From the very way he handled it, there was no mistaking the tender admiration he felt for its owner. He also took out four fathoms of rope, too: lashed one end to the handle, the other to his belt. Then he began doggedly to climb. 'I would advise haste, *esploratori piccoli*,' he confided gently, his voice almost soundless after the ferocity of Captain Pan. 'There are Roarers all around.'

That was all it took. The Explorers belted tight their blanket coats and clambered into the trees, like sailors swarming up rigging towards a crow's nest among the stars.

The climb was exhausting. Thin boughs snapped under

their feet. Fir needles pricked at them. Bark came loose under their fingers and the smell of resin made them dizzy. Worst of all, the oozing gum within the trees smothered them in stickiness, gave them webbed fingers and glued their knees together. Pine needles stuck to their arms and legs and hair until they were furry with fir. At first only single wasps cruised by, curious, clumsy, buffeting the children's faces, buzzing in their ears. But when the shaking of the tree dislodged a hive from its crevice, tens and hundreds of wasps poured out of it and gathered round in clouds, drawn to gummy faces, sticking to open palms.

'*Owowo! I got stung!*'

And crane-flies came, too, and gnats and horseflies and bluebottles and ladybirds. The children's shadows caught and stuck fast to the welling gum, pulling them up short, threatening to tangle their feet in darkness.

Curly made the mistake of looking down and saw that the land beneath had shrunk with distance to the size of a pocket garden. John made the mistake of looking up, and saw that the tree tops were almost reached and above those was nothing but grey rock and snow. They dragged themselves on to a narrow ledge of rock, and lay there, noses over the brink, too tired to close their eyelids. So they saw the Ravelling Man make his slow ascent.

In among the branches, his tangle of clothing would have snagged on every twig and splinter and unravelled him to his backbone. So he avoided the monkey-puzzle trees and climbed the sheer rock face instead—not nimbly, not fast, but with a stolid determination—*step, balance, pull*. The heavy sea chest swung from the back of his belt like the pendulum of a clock: *tick tock, tick tock*. Reaching their perch, he carefully, carefully laid himself along the narrow shelf of rock. Wendy had the curious compulsion to reach out and touch that strange woolly pelt. She caught the smell of snake's eggs, cough drops, and lion.

'Will the Roarers come after us, Mr Ravello?' she asked.

'No, miss. I think not.'

'And will there be food?' asked the Second Twin.

'Undoubtedly. Eagle's eggs. Mountain cucumbers. And manna.'

'Manna?'

'Mannas good and bad. Be careful which you eat. Mannas maketh man, but only the good kind.'

'How do you know these things, Mr Ravello, sir?' asked Curly.

Ravello began hauling up the sea chest, hand-over-hand. They could hear his clenched teeth grinding with the effort of it. 'Oh, I am a travelling man, *pequeño marquis*. I listen out. I listen in.'

The last of the wasps sank down and away, like swimmers realizing they are out of their depth.

Clip. Clip. Instead, pebbles began to rattle through the

branches of the trees, then to hit the ledge. *Clip. Clip.* Soon some began to hit the Explorers—*ow! ouch!*—and they realized that they were under attack from something bigger than wasps. Huge grey birds with scraggy legs and claws like sugar tongs were circling overhead, dropping stones to dislodge the intruders. This ledge was the birds' evening perch, and they meant to keep it for themselves. The stones rattled down like hailstones. A cold wind blew.

Tootles sniffed loudly and put into words what everybody was thinking. 'This is no fun any more.'

Sometimes a game takes over from the person who thought of it. In Neverland games always do, and play isn't play: it's real—which is wonderful and makes your brain spin zigger-zag behind your eyes and sends little jets of hotness through your stomach and steals the spit out of your mouth; and all the birds are harpies and all the logs are cannon and all the curtains are ghosts and all the noises are monsters . . . It's the best of moments, and you know you will remember it for ever.

But, by Skylights, it's scary!

Peter Pan rose to his knees, white shirt blustering around him, long dark hair standing on end in the wind. There was the most wonderful smile on his face. 'My friends—my band of brothers—we came here . . .'

'And sisters!' said Tootles peevishly.

'And sisters, of course. We came here to be Explorers. To

be treasure-seekers. Yes? What did we think? That it would
be easy? That it would be safe? Look there! Look!' And
they looked where he was pointing, out across the
landscape they had crossed, lush and green in the distance,
harsh and bare close to; a trackless wilderness of hardships
and toil. 'Did we think the trails would be well trodden?
No. But we did it! Did we think that ordinary everybodies
came here every day of the week? No, none but the likes of
us! Did we want to do something easy? Did we want a walk
in the park?' They looked at him with his fists raised above
his head, the wind clenched between his white teeth, his
collarbones like two wings above his heart. The skin of his
wrists was lined with white scars where tiny slivers of metal
had flown from the blades of two swords as he and Jas.
Hook fought it out to the death. He was magnificent.

'But we are not like you, Peter!' cried Curly. 'Some of us
get tired—and scared.'

'Supposing the treasure's not worth it, after all this?'
said John.

'Then it would not be treasure,' murmured Ravello with
undeniable logic.

'Not everyone can be rich,' Peter went on. 'Not
everyone can be strong or clever. Not everyone can be
beautiful. But we can *all* be brave! If we tell ourselves we
can do it; if we say to our hearts, "Don't jump about"; if we
carry ourselves like heroes . . . we can all be brave! We can

all look Danger in the face and be glad to meet it, and draw our swords and say, "Have at you, Danger! You don't scare me!" Courage is just there for the taking: you don't need money to buy it. You don't need to go to school to learn it! Courage is the thing, isn't it? Don't you think so, people? Aren't I right? Courage is the thing! All goes if courage goes!'

Earlier in the day, no one would have taken one step more for the boy who called them scupper-rats and mutineers and threatened them with stranding and short rations. Now, though, if Peter Pan had asked it, any one of them would have walked out on to the wing of an airborne aeroplane or leapt off the highest diving board into a glass of milk. They brushed the pine needles off their limbs, sucked the wasp-stings out of their skin, and prepared to scramble onwards up the rocky mountainside.

Ravello kindly produced a knife and cut loose the Darlings' sticky shadows—'Now they won't catch as you climb'—and put the shadows into the sea chest for safe-keeping. Puppy must have thought the cutting hurt, because it rushed in and seized hold of Ravello's garment in its sharp little teeth, and began to pull for all it was worth. Whole hanks of wool came away and began to unravel, exposing a strangely knobbly, mottled, scuffed boot. The circus-master reached out with lightning speed and, grabbing Puppy round the throat, held it up close to his face. The children feared for it—thought Ravello must be about to bite its nose or hurl it off the cliff. But he only looked into the creature's bulgy little eyes and whispered a few gentle words: asked, 'Animal. Do you have the smallest desire ever to grow up and be a big dog?' Puppy took this to heart and stopped chewing on him. It said a lot for Ravello's powers as an animal trainer.

He also persuaded Pan back into the scarlet frock coat— 'It is the colour of bravery, sir; it will encourage the others.' Then he whetted his knife on a stone and reached for the sticky, tattered darkness around Peter's feet.

'*I keep my shadow!*' Peter snarled, stamping on Ravello's blade.

The valet snatched his crushed hand to his body but did not protest. It would have been a brave man who wrangled with such a Boy.

CHAPTER FIFTEEN
Nowhereland

Slightly had been banished to Nowhereland where no one would speak a word to him. Of course Fireflyer had been banished there too, so there was nothing to stop him doing it.

'*We hate 'em, don't we?*' said the fairy, who had taken to calling him (now that he was taller) Mr 'Slightly-more'.

'Hmm,' said Slightly doubtfully. He had never quite got the hang of hating people and now that he was bigger it did not seem quite honourable to hate anyone smaller than he was. They were sitting at the foot of Neverpeak Mountain, chewing empty honeycombs filched from the trees by the light-fingered fairy.

'We'd like to cut 'em up for firewood, wouldn't we?' said Fireflyer.

'Probably not,' said Slightly, though he would have appreciated the firewood: it was getting very cold. The honeycombs did not even touch the edges of his hunger. Fireflyer could get by, eating musical notes, but Slightly (if he hadn't been Slightly and as gentle as a lamb) would have gladly killed somebody for a prawn sandwich.

'I suppose we never shall get to see what treasure is in Hook's treasure chest. What would you have wished for it to be, Fireflyer?'

'Sherbet-flavoured eyeballs!' answered Fireflyer quick as a wink (though he might have been lying, of course).

Oddly, the taller Slightly grew, the further back he remembered, so that now he could picture Cadogan Square again, and Kensington Gardens—even, once upon a time, a piano teacher who held pen-nibs under his wrists to make him arch them. (That was why he had taken up the clarinet.) Slightly-more could even remember his first time in Neverland . . .

'Tell me a story,' demanded Fireflyer.

'Why? Do you eat them too, then?'

'Only the ohs and ayes and ees and oos. The kays are too spikey and the zeds are too buzzy and the ones with the dots get stuck in your teeth and the esses sometimes slide down inside your vest and tickle. Oh, and make it a happy ending, Mr Slightly-more, or I'll get a pain.'

So Slightly put the pleasant warmth of Fireflyer in his

shirt pocket—*'Oh, and be sure there's a fairy in it!'*—and told him the story running through his mind at that moment.

'One day the pirates found Peter Pan's underground den and lay in wait and captured us Lost Boys one by one as we climbed out; also Wendy and Michael and John. But they couldn't catch Pan because he was fast asleep inside the den and didn't come out. So the dastardly Jas. Hook took out a bottle of poison (never went anywhere without one) and trickled some down into Peter's medicine so that he would drink it when he woke and DIE!'

'I'm getting a pain,' warned Fireflyer.

'. . . But the fairy Tinker Bell, who was loyal and true and brave, saw it happen and knew what she had to do!'

'Was she clever, then, this Tinker Bell?'

'Simply brilliant. Don't interrupt.'

'And beautiful?'

'In a whitish, waspish way. Can I go on?'

'And female?'

'Very. Do you want this story or not?'

'And a liar?'

'She said once that Wendy was a bird and that Peter wanted us to shoot her dead.'

The lie was so huge that it silenced even Fireflyer.

'Peter woke up and was just about to drink the poison when Tinker Bell up and drank it instead, and so . . .'

'Ow! Ow! Ow! Why did you have to tell me that? Ah! I have a terrible pain! Ow, I hate stories!'

'. . . And Tinker Bell *almost* died but *didn't*, because she was too much loved, and so Peter chased after Hook and crept aboard the *Jolly Roger* and freed us captives and fought Hook with thrust and parry and lunge—*huh! huh! have at you!*—and drove him to the ship's rail and tipped him over . . . *tick tick tick* . . . right into the jaws of the crocodile!'

. . . *dile!* . . . *dile!* . . . *dile!* The tail end of the story lashed to and fro between the rock faces of Neverpeak: an echo of marvellous menace.

'Woohoo!' Fireflyer was so excited that a small burn appeared in Slightly's shirt pocket. *'Boo to Hook and down to the bottom with him!'*

'I don't know that it is quite the thing to triumph over a man you never knew,' said Slightly sternly.

'Why not? Didn't Hook deserve it? Wasn't he a villain and a blackguard and a do-no-good sticky-ender?'

Slightly had to admit Hook was. 'And very *loud*, as I remember,' he said creasing his forehead. 'He shouted at his men all the time and threatened them and swaggered and blustered and thought he was no end of a dog and that there was no one to match him in all Neverland.'

A little voice said, *'Just like Peter, you mean?'*

'Quiet, Fireflyer! You don't know what you are talking about!'

The fairy peeped nervously out, his mouth a small round O of surprise. *'But I didn't say anything, Mr Slightly-more.'*

And Slightly had to admit it then: that the voice had not come from his shirt pocket at all, but from inside his own heart; a treacherous, mutinous little voice that was still telling him even now, over and over again: Peter Pan had begun to behave *exactly* like Captain Hook.

The sun went down like a bacon-slicer, and the night was as dark as black pudding. Or so it seemed to a boy cut off from his supper. Slightly-more's thoughts were darker still, as he lay with his eyes tight shut, and tried to sleep. For he had realized something truly dreadful: an idea that settled like hot sparks on his forehead.

'You know those other people I spotted from on high when we were playing?' called Fireflyer through the darkness, in a loud whisper.

'Go to sleep, Fireflyer.'

'But I told you about them, remember?'

'What, the Aztecs and Incas?'

'No. The others. The lurkers and underbrushy ambushers. Remember?'

'No,' said Slightly firmly. He did not want to play the game again. He wanted to go to sleep where there would be no cold draughts, no painful ideas falling like sparks on his forehead. 'You tell lovely lies, dear,' he said, not wishing to be unkind, 'but tell them in the morning, if you please.'

Unluckily, Fireflyer was not lying.

And the sparks falling on Slightly's forehead were as real as the foot now resting on his hip, the hand now closing around his throat. He opened his eyes to find two dozen hulking boys brandishing clubs and burning bulrushes.

'Let's spit him and roast him and eat him!' said one.

Slightly reached for his clarinet, as a mother might reach for her child. But they mistook it for a weapon and kicked it away into the mud. They kicked Slightly, too.

'You're in the League. You're one of *his*. Saw you with him.'

A surge of pride went through Slightly before he remembered: he was not in the League of Pan at all; he was just a boy who had grown too long in the arms and legs, and been banished. 'You shouldn't be speaking to me,' he said. 'I've been sent to Nowhereland.' (Slightly, knowing nothing about the Roarers, still did not realize what danger he was in.)

'Speak to you? Blagh,' grunted a huge youth with ragged earlobes. 'Kill you is all.'

A fairy wanting to live on the *ohs* and *ayes* and *oos* and *ees* of the Roarers would soon starve, because having grown into young men, they hardly spoke at all. Now they believed they had captured one of Pan's party, and a murderous light burned in their eyes. They lived for the day when they would ambush Peter Pan himself and be revenged for their bigness and banishment. In the meantime they were willing to settle for killing one of his League of Explorers. Ravello had spoken true when he said they were worse than pirates, less tameable than bears, entirely heartless.

'Where's Pan? Say or die!' said the oldest Roarer.

Just then, Fireflyer jumped up out of Slightly's shirt pocket and ate the wax out of a Roarer's ear. *'Peter Pan? Peter Pan? We hate him, don't we, Mr Slightly-more!'*

'He has gone up the mountain,' said Slightly, not seeing any harm in telling them.

'To fetch us our treasure!' piped Firefly, feeling a nice lie was called for. *'We made him go.'*

'Treasure?' (The word has magic no matter how tall you have grown.)

'We want to chop 'em up for firewood,' suggested Fireflyer enthusiastically.

And so somehow the Roarers got the idea that Slightly and Co. were dogging Peter Pan's trail, as intent on killing him as they were. They also got wind of a treasure, and they liked the sound of that. Folding their gangling long legs under them, they sat down on the ground, each boy taking care not to brush his bare arms against another's. (Slightly thought they would be warmer if they huddled together, but then he was new to this adolescence business.) One by one, their bulrushes burned out.

For a while they sat in silence, then at last Slightly could not help asking the question gnawing away at his heart. 'Why did *you* people grow big?' he said. 'Do you know?'

They shrugged their big bony shoulders. 'Pan poisoned us, of course.'

'Poisoned everyone.'

'Poisoned everywhere.'

'Oh, I don't think . . .' began Slightly.

But the Long Lost Boys were adamant. During the wild and comfortless years of their exile they had all come to believe this one version of history:

Once upon a time, at the beginning of the end, when it was always summer, Peter Pan took out a bottle of poison and poured it into the Lagoon. First the cuttlefish died and then the mermaids. The turquoise waves grew bigger— much bigger—turned grey, then white-haired with foam. On dry land the summer trees blushed red and dropped their leaves. The poison bleached the colour out of the sun, leached the sap out of the flowers, the song out of the birds. Time moved on, where it was never meant to. Even the weather began to grow bigger: breezes turned into huge winds, felling trees and totem poles. In the sky little wisps of mare's-tails grew into great clumsy clouds lumpy with thunder and lightning. The fairies, fizzed up by the electricity in the air, went to war with one another.

'And he poisoned us too, when we weren't looking, and made us grow, then turned us out for getting big, and sent us to Nowhereland same as you.' The sentence was all the sadder for being the longest any Roarer had yet spoken.

Slightly swallowed hard. 'Who told you all this?'

Again the shrug. Again the lips pushed out, the eyes shifting behind half-closed lids. Their fingers scuffed up stones, which they threw at the mountain, as if at Peter Pan himself.

'Somebody.'

Each said something to the same effect.

'Some man.'

'Some traveller I met.'

'Gave me a job for a while.'

'Me too. Till the fire.'

'A travelling man.'

Something cold kissed Slightly's cheek. A flake of snow. Something colder than snow settled on his heart. As he got to his feet, the seam of his blanket coat, too small now even to reach his elbows, strained and split. He felt dizzy, either from the swirling of the snow round his head or the fear gripping his heart. 'I must go up the mountain,' he said. 'Will someone show me the way?'

'To kill Pan?' said one, eagerly raising himself up on his elbows.

'Mmm,' said Slightly. 'Where should I start the climb?'

But even for the fearsome Roarers, the mountain was

beyond bounds, a place of unimaginable danger. They had never dared to set foot there.

'Is it such a fearful place, then, Neverpeak?' said Slightly trembling despite his resolve.

'You said there's treasure up there,' said a youth through a dirty stain of a beard. 'D'you think it would still be there, if any had ever climbed up there and lived?'

'Neverpeak?' said another, talking aloud to himself. 'Is that what he called it? Every man else calls it by a different name.'

Every man else called it The Point of No Return.

CHAPTER SIXTEEN
Shadow Boxing

It is perfectly true that without their shadows the Explorers felt light-of-heart at first, and happy: even when the snow began, and little avalanches of scree swept down and sliced at their knees. Soon they would be at the top, and Hook's treasure would be theirs! What would it be? Cloth-of-gold or Turkish Delight? Silver pistols or horse bridles in red morocco leather? The crowns of sixteen eastern potentates? The keys to a glass palace?

Storybooks? thought Wendy to herself.

'Do you remember,' said Tootles blithely. 'Mother used to call us *her* dearest treasure!'

'And Papa said he should keep us in his bank, because we were worth more than all the money in the world!'

Wendy glanced quickly at Peter, knowing how much he hated such talk. Whenever there was mention of mothers, he would look at his hands and flex his fingers. Once those fingers had tugged and tugged on a cold brass handle, rapped at a window pane, prised in vain at a lock. Just once, lonely for home, Peter had flown home from Neverland, only to find the bedroom window shut. He had never forgiven his mother for closing it.

Luckily, though, Peter was not listening. He was too busy climbing, hauling himself higher by the strength of his arms alone. Now and then, his feet floated clear of the ground, like a diver exploring a reef, but it was not what you could call flying—not real flying—and his poor hands were cut and bleeding. At last, with a groan of exhaustion, he came to rest face-down on the cold rock, clawing feebly over one shoulder, clutching for the hem of his own shadow. All the strength seemed to be going out of him.

'Did you say it would be easier without my shadow, Ravello?'

'Far easier, *bellissimo generalissimo*. It is a well known fact: at this altitude shadows double their weight.'

'Do it, then! Be rid of it! It's a nuisance and it weighs me down and I never liked it!'

In one lithe movement, in one painless motion, with a

blade not even visible within the sleeve of his cardigan, Ravello sliced away Peter's shadow. As he folded it neatly in four places and laid it delicately in the sea chest, he crooned his own soft-spoken thoughts on the subject of mothers. (Ravello seemed to have an equally low opinion of the breed.)

'We are all better off without 'em. After all's said and done, what is a mother good for but to blight a chap's life? Oh, in her striped gown with the skirts drawn up behind and her neck like a swan, she may draw envious looks from a boy's cohort. She may look very well sipping a glass of champagne on the Headmaster's lawn. But when the grass is too wet for her to sit and watch a Dry Bob in the fives court or opening the batting or playing flying man, or the river bank beside the Raft is too muddy for her boots to let her watch a Wet Bob standing proud and steady in Dreadnought during Procession, and when on Wall Day she is too busy at her dressmaker's—or laughs merrily at the news a boy has failed his colours and ended up in Rowland instead of Schoolyard, and when she sends no encouraging good wishes before the épée bouts . . . well then, a chap's undone, wouldn't you say? Or when at June Speeches a lad looks out from the rostrum, with the words of Ovid on his lips, conned at the greatest pains, ready to recite before the entire Upper, and finds no mother there . . . though even that is better than when, on a rare visit, she praises mathematics and slights those things her boy excels at, such as his boxing and beagling, and asks only after his Grammar and French declensions and what he knows of the Etruscans. Nay, I tell you, mothers would sooner have for a son a Slack Bob sent up for good for parsing and conjugating, than a batsman who hits four sixes an over on the Threepenny or bowls a maiden on the Sixpenny! And when finally, despite discouragement, all's to play for and Fate puts in his hand a Pop cane and the clouds stand ready to open and shower their glory on a boy's head, and show him the best, and award him the very silver and shining proof of his excellence . . . is it supportable to *call him hence to save on musketry and boating bills and school fees?* And fuss and fret and tap an impatient shoe and bin his ribbon lists while the poor sinner packs up his bags tormented the while by the sound through the open window of willow on leather and the cheering-on of runners, and the clash of blades and the whistle of javelins and the deuce knows what else . . . ? Ach! Worlds have been lost by the heartlessness of mothers. Whole worlds, I tell you! Whole worlds!'

The crooning had risen to a roar. When at last their silence impressed itself on Ravello, he looked round and found all the Explorers staring at him.

'What language is he talking?' asked John. 'Is it Esquimeau?'

But Wendy went over to Ravello, where he crouched beside the sea chest arranging and re-arranging its contents until everything lay in perfect order. She laid a hand on his heaving shoulder, feeling the greasy coarseness of the bunchy wool tremble. 'Are you by any chance a Lost Boy, sir?'

'Certainly not!' Ravello jumped to his feet with startling grace. 'By no means, miss! No! No no. I am not. Most certainly not.'

'Has anyone seen Puppy?' asked Curly.

As soon as they woke next morning, the children glanced nervously at their cuffs and calves, to check that they had not sprouted in the night. Like Slightly. Hard going as their journey was, any hardship was preferable to being cast out on Neverpeak, shunned for growing bigger. Like Slightly. Why had it happened to Slightly and not to them? Not Knowing was the worst and most worrying part. They decided that it was, almost certainly, because Slightly had been wearing adult clothing when he arrived in Neverland.

Clothes are so much part of what a person is, after all.

The route to the summit was up chimneys of rock and over ridges of snow. They would scrabble up slopes of slippery marble only to slide back down, dislodging each other into a bruised and breathless pile, and have to set off all over again. Threads of iron and coal and fossils laced the rocks together. Ravines cracked them apart again, so that the explorers often found themselves on the brink of a precipice, looking down into bottomless nothingness.

'Has *anyone* seen Puppy?' asked Curly yet again, and yet again they searched and searched, finding nothing. Yet again they called—'Puppy! Come, Puppy!'—but the corniches of snow that loomed over their heads creaked and groaned and sagged in swags, as if they might fall at the next vibration.

'He'll be waiting for us at the bottom, when we get down again,' said Wendy brightly, so that the littler ones would not cry, but she bit her lip when she remembered the crevasses and rockslides, the wasps and gummy trees. Neverpeak was no place for a tiny little puppy dog.

The changes that had altered Neverland's forests and hills had changed Neverpeak too. Once, sweet-water springs had sent glittering tails of spray flickering down tapestries of wild flowers and birds' nests. Now ice welled up from the core of the mountain, splitting it open and spilling glaciers down it like grimy grey lava. The glaciers bulldozed boulders into teetering towers of rock. Nearing one such glacier, the explorers felt a wall of sudden cold: such a solid wall that they could have drawn pictures on it if they had just had a crayon.

'How shall we ever be warm again?' asked First Twin through chattering teeth.

'Hot tea and muffins,' said Second Twin, 'when we get down.'

'How shall we ever get down?' said Tootles.

'Slow and steady,' said Peter with a careless laugh, 'or very fast indeed, if you slip!'

Here and there, a sugar coating of white snow covered the dirty grey ice, hiding the huge cracks that threatened to swallow foolhardy travellers. It wound like a highway towards the peak, and Peter started up it without a backward glance, so that the others felt bound to follow. But the cold struck through their shoes and chilled the marrow in their shins, their thighbones, their hips, their spines, their shoulderblades. Ravello roped them all together like proper mountaineers, but Peter would not be tied, refused to be tied.

'Only think of the treasure up top!' he said, and his breath was dragony with the cold. 'Only think of *my treasure!*' His loudness brought a rustling rush of snow down from the mountainside to wash across their feet and wipe out their footprints.

Suddenly everyone came to a halt. Out over a yawning ravine the glacier shrank to a thin beam of ice, like a bridge of cheap, crazed glass. It was so slippery that the Darlings got down on hands and knees to crawl across it. It was so thin that they could see right through to Certain Death below.

'Is this a proper quest we are on?' asked Tootles. 'A person could get killed!'

Peter gave a savage grin, scrambled to his feet . . . and strode out across the narrow ice-bridge, shouting, 'A quest, Tootles? Yes! To be or not to be. *That* is the quest!' The others looked on, open-mouthed. '*Come on, then, all of you! Courage is the thing. All goes if courage goes!*'

He was within a few paces of the other side when he looked down and, there in the shiny ice, caught sight of something that broke his stride, broke his nerve. Peter gave a cry so terrible that all the harpy birds left the mountain then and there, never to return. For the space of a few heartbeats, pandemonium raged inside him. Then, foolishly, he tried to run. His boot soles skidded, his arms went out, and he pitched on his face . . . and over the edge of the ice-bridge.

Ravello gave a cry, threw aside the rope he was holding and went—*hop*—one—*skip*—two—*jump*—three— '*I'm coming, sir!*'—to where Peter hung by his fingers from the icicles beneath the ice-bridge. Ravello's weight smashed a hole in the bridge, and he dropped feet-first through it, saved only from plummeting to his death by arms flung wide and the width of his great woolly shoulders. 'Grab my legs, boy!' he told Peter. 'Grab hold!'

'I saw him!' came Peter's voice from beneath the bridge. 'I saw Hook!'

Ravello's body, gripped by the ice, writhed with cold. 'His memory, perhaps. His likeness printed on the air.'

'No, no!' The small voice was full of panic and confusion. 'I saw my reflection in the ice and it was . . .' The icicles within Peter's palm were ready to melt or snap. Soon he would plunge into the ravine below. But the memory of that reflection troubled him almost more. For ice is a true mirror. In it he had seen the long ringlets Ravello had coiled into his hair, seen the sunburn darkening his skin, seen the red coat and thigh boots.

'Take hold of my legs, sir! I shall pull you up.'

'I can't fly. Why can't I, Ravello? Why can't I fly?'

The circus-master started to slip, reached to anchor himself—with the gristly crunch of a blade—and kept his grip. Peter Pan transferred his weight from the icicles to Ravello's legs. 'Cling tight, sir, or you may pull off my boots and still fall!'

Not that Pan weighed more than a pillow full of feathers. But it still cost Ravello a titanic effort to pull his body and legs and boots and Peter up through the hole and into the circle of his arms, safe at last.

'Why can't I fly, Ravello? Why?'

'All in good time, sir,' purred Ravello soothingly.

Peter's fingers sank deep in the woolly hide as he tried

to push his valet away. 'Don't touch me! I mustn't be touched! Go back and get that sea chest, valet!' But his hands got caught.

Ravello carefully, carefully extricated each of Pan's icy fingers from the woollen tangles and chafed them warm. His voice was a coaxing whisper. 'And just what is this treasure we so assiduously seek, sir?'

Pan looked towards the peak. A few more hours of climbing lay ahead, but already Peter knew what the treasure chest stowed there would contain. Who had put the knowledge into his head he could not tell, and yet there it was, along with memories of a place he had never been and a delight he could not contain. 'I don't know what you call them, but they are so shiny and fine and I have wanted them for so LONG!'

Ravello gave a blissful sigh. With four fathoms of rope and with infinite care, he coaxed the other Explorers across the ice-bridge, then the sea chest too, on its bouncy pram wheels. Just as those wheels reached the place where Peter had fallen through and been pulled to safety, there was a loud *Crack!* and the whole ice-bridge crumbled and dropped into the ravine. The falling sea chest all but took Ravello with it, but with a guttural, choking roar he withstood the shock and kept hold of the rope, and saved both chest and himself from falling to destruction.

The Darlings all ran to help him, and together they hauled up the dead weight of a sea chest swinging and twirling on its rope like a hanged man. They found Ravello laughing to himself—on and on—a wry, self-mocking laugh, a noise like water welling into the bottom of a boat.

CHAPTER SEVENTEEN
Not Himself

In Neverland, a treasure chest contains the treasure-seeker's dearest wish, the thing he or she wants more than anything else in the world. Those who had wished for gold doubloons and pieces of nine and ten, those who had thought of tiaras, necklaces, and pocket watches; those who had hoped for storybooks and Fabergé eggs no longer wanted any of those things. All they wanted now was a warm fire and a hot meal, a feather eiderdown and some steaming Bovril. True, Curly did desperately wish he had not lost the puppy, but quickly unthought the wish; a puppy shut up in a treasure chest was not at all a happy thought.

But it made no difference what they wished. They all knew that Peter would wish better than any of them, and that *he* would decide what they found when they finally lifted the lid of Hook's treasure chest.

They sang to carry them the last little way, and the rainbow banner fluttered bravely over their heads.

'To the top, we're going right to the top;
From the capital letter to the last full stop;
From the very first sip to the final drop:
That's where we're going: right to the top!

All the way we're going; we're going all the way,
From the first crack of dawn to the close of the day.
No matter what the scaredy-cats and don't-believers say
That's where we're going: we're going all the way!

We've come through wind and fire and through cold sea spray;
We fought off dragons and we kept the bears at bay;
They wouldn't dare to stay and stand and fight us anyway!
Cos they know where we're going: we're going all the way.'

'But we didn't fight off dragons and bears—not really,' said First Twin.

'But we could have!' said Second.

'All the way we're going; we're going all the way:
Right from Sunday morning up to Saturday,
Eating flying fish on the road to Mandalay!
All the way we're going; we're going all the way!
And if you don't believe us, we're going anyway!
We're going all the way, we are! We're going all the way!'

And before they knew it, there they were, with nowhere further up to go. The sides of the mountain fell away from them like the skirts of a king's robe, and their heads were crowned with cloud.

From the top of Neverpeak you can see beyond Belief: over every obstacle, over the heads of the oldest, tallest anyone; as far back as you choose to remember, and as far as wherever you mean to go next. You can see where you went wrong and what a long way you've come. You can look down on your enemies and overcome your fears. The whole world looks up to a child on the summit of Neverpeak! Now the Explorers stood on the snowy crest and surveyed the whole island, pointing out landmarks to one another. They could see the distant Neverwood, charred and still smoking. They could see the distant yellow Lagoon and the narrow strait leading out into the wild ocean. The course they had sailed aboard the *Jolly Peter* was still written in the ocean: a white foamy furrow looping out and round and ending in a shatter of wreckage out at Lodestone Rock. They could see Grief Reef and the stripy rockscape that hid the Maze of Witches.

'Oh look, Peter! Look!' cried Wendy. 'There are the trees where you found us berries for breakfast!'

But Peter had no eyes for the view. He was scouring the mountaintop for the Treasure, kicking up clouds of snow, groaning with weariness and cold and frustration. The treasure map flapped itself to tatters in his hands. 'Where is it? Where *is* it?' he muttered over and over again.

Since Neverland's slow slide from summer into winter, snow had settled on Neverpeak where none had lain before. Deep drifts of softness had rounded its rocky summit into a white dome hiding the Treasure promised on the map.

'May I help you look, sir?' called Ravello, always slower than the children and only now nearing the top.

'NO! You can't come up here!' Peter shouted back. 'This is MY place! You can't come up here!'

'No,' said the circus-master, as if this was the simple truth. 'No, I know,' and he contented himself with studying the landscape laid out below, intently looking, looking, looking and cocking his head to listen, too.

Pan dug in the snow with his swordfish sword until its sawtooth edge was worn smooth.

'Cold,' said Ravello, which was no more than the truth.

Peter dug with a piece of slate, shovelling up snow until he was white-haired from his own digging.

'Warmer,' said Ravello . . . which was absurd.

Peter dug with his bare hands, because they were already too cold to feel the pain of it.

'Hotter,' said Ravello from his perch lower down.

And then a hollow sound, a smooth hardness that did not skin his knuckles, a streak of red beneath the snow. The Treasure was found!

There was a big padlock, but Wendy came with her sword, and, with their four hands on the hilt—oh, how cold Peter's were!—they forced open the hasp. Then Peter Pan stepped up on to the curved lid and raised his two fists in the air, tossed back his head of dark and glossy curls, and *crowed*.

'Avaaaaast!!'

It was a noise part-lark, part-hawk. It was a shout of triumph and an avenging war cry. It was part choirboy, part delinquent. Whatever it was, it was not a cock-a-doodle, and it ended in a spluttering cough.

'*Hot!*' whispered Ravello, and closed his eyes in an ecstasy of joy.

The lid rose, and with it the wind, so that a column of twisted snow eddied all around. Even those who had thought they were too tired and cold to care what the chest contained found themselves wishing and wishing that it might contain their heart's desire.

'WHAT?!' Peter uttered a cry of dismay and plunged in his hands, hurling aside twigs and dry grass and peat. First Twin had wished for warmth, so here was the fuel to build a fire.

Peter put his hands to his head in despair, and his hands were covered in a glitter that was not snow. Wendy had wished for fairy dust, to help them fly home again, so here was fairy dust.

There were dry tea-leaves and bread dough, cold spaghetti and sago pudding all loose in among everything else, because the Twins had wished when they were hungry.

There were the regular treasure-chest things—gold doubloons and bags of diamonds, because John Darling had not been able to imagine a treasure chest containing anything different. And Tootles's tiara was there after all, and a few yards of Indian silk.

Puppy, puppy, puppy! thought Curly, but it was too late to wish the lost dog into Hook's treasure chest. Curly blamed himself that somewhere, out on the bleak glaciers and murrains, a tiny wee puppy was wandering about lost because he had not wished soon enough.

Even Puppy (wherever he was now) must have been better at wishing than Curly, because there was a juicy marrow-bone stuck in the hinge. Just no Puppy to eat it.

But though they had been expecting wonders of some sort, *no one* could understand why *TINKER BELL* was there!

In a corner of the lid, cocooned in gossamer, emerging like a butterfly from its chrysalis, a lovely, lissom fairy no bigger than a child's hand, stirred into wakefulness, complaining sleepily that someone had left open a window. *'How can a person sleep in such a draught?'* She blinked once, then once again. *'Peter? Is that you, Peter Pan?'*

The Darlings were enchanted. They took it in turns to hold the fairy in the palm of a hand. 'We thought you must be dead at your age!' said Tootles (which Wendy felt was not quite tactful).

'So I was,' said Tinker Bell, *'or hibernating. It's hard to tell.'* Then she complained that their hands were all far too cold to sit on, and that Peter was ignoring her. *'Fairies die if you ignore them, you know!'*

'Peter, look!' cried Wendy. 'It's Tinker Bell! Did you wish for her to be here? Is *she* your treasure?' It gave her the oddest feeling to think it. But after all, it was very noble of Peter to prize a friend above gold, silver, or honey sandwiches.

But Peter continued to rummage in the treasure chest, casting aside a storybook, crushing a painted egg.

Tinker Bell looked again. *'Oh,'* she said sleepily. *'I thought it was Peter Pan, but it is not he. It is the Other one.'* And she went back to sleep.

And there at last, filling fully half the chest, lay the Real Treasure—the one for which they had risked everything, the one which had brought them here to the Point of No Return. Peter lifted them out with gentle hands: a cup, a trophy, a cane, a statuette, a top hat, a plaque shaped like a knight's shield, a cap circled with rings of red and white, an oar painted blue-green at the paddle, which he clutched lovingly to his chest.

Wendy picked up a trophy, its base engraved with fifty names and the words, SPENCER CUP FOR RIFLE 1894. 'It is very pretty, Peter, but why?' Peter did not answer, but snatched up another and looked at it, a chalice plated in shiny silver.

Curly was dragging together the kindling into a bonfire. With every moment, the views to north, south, east, and west were melting away, licked up by tongues of flying snow. A blizzard was closing in. John called Ravello to bring a match, to light the fire.

But Peter went on gazing at the cup in his hands, shivers shaking him from head to foot. His look of rapture turned to one of horror as he saw, looking back at him, his own reflection. It was the same one he had seen in the ice-bridge. Reaching sideways, he took hold of Wendy's hand.

'I am not myself,' he said in a whisper. 'Wendy . . . I . . . am . . . not . . . me.'

The figure of Peter Pan's valet just then emerged on to the peak of the mountain. With the weather worsening, it seemed an odd time to push back his hood. His features were hidden now only by the flurrying snow.

'Ah! Over here, Ravello!' called John. 'A match, if you please!'

Ravello did not seem to hear, though he had heard Peter well enough. 'Not yourself, did you say? Oh true! How true! You have not been yourself for the past ten leagues.' Again that laugh, like a rising tide swamping a beach. 'Not yourself, no. For you have become Hook. Captain Hook. Captain Jas. Hook, scourge of Neverland!'

The name alone sank into their chests like a steel hook. Ravello walked over to the treasure chest, gently picked up one of the cups, held it to his cheek and kissed it, long and tender. He also took the opportunity to give Peter a push with the sole of his boot.

'Here is the proof,' he said hugging the trophy. 'Behold the Treasure—the selfsame Treasure Captain Hook left here all those years ago! Are these boys' toys? No. Do they smack of the Cock-a-doodle? No! Only Hook, with his iron will—his flinty soul—his steely determination—could find the same Treasure he left here all those years ago! See, then, how I groomed you for the role, boy! See how I readied you for this moment! See how I coached you into wishing the right wishes, and finding the right Treasure! But oh, you made it so easy for me! So ridiculously easy! What a service you did me, Pan, of your own free will! What a loving-kindness you did me the day you put on my second-best jacket!'

CHAPTER EIGHTEEN
Taking Deadness

'*HOOK!*'

The circus-master flinched and gave a shudder from nose to tail, as a dog will whose ears get wet. 'Once, but no longer,' he said. 'I am the man who *once was Hook*. Look there, if you would see Hook!' And he pointed at Peter Pan with the iron hook he wore in place of a right hand. 'See where he wears the red jacket! See where his hair falls in coils to his shoulders! You of all people should know: if you put on another's clothes, you become that man!'

Peter's frozen fingers fumbled for the buttons of the red

frock coat (Hook's second-best frock coat) and slipped his arms out of its sleeves. Despite the icy blast wrapping the mountain in coils of cold as jagged as barbed wire, the jacket dropped to the ground behind him and his flimsy tunic rattled round him in the wind.

Ravello laughed. 'You may shed the coat, but not the man you are become! No one but an Eton boy can unfasten the old school tie!' And it was true that however hard Peter wrenched at the white tie round his throat, he could not slip its knot. 'How willingly you let me comb the imagination out of your head! How readily you let me help you back into the coat each time you shed its scarlet magic. But I see your friends doubt me, Pan! So tell them! Tell them! Tell them how you have dreamed Hook's dreams—remembered Hook's memories—felt his boyhood disappointments, given in to his temper!' He began to load cups and trophies, caps and ribbons into the big pockets of his peculiar garment. 'You are become James Hook, and here is the proof! These were the things dearest to his heart, and only YOU could wish them here! *That* is why I needed you.'

'No! No! I am Pan!' protested Peter, tugging off the shiny leather boots. 'I shall always be young and there is no one like me! I am the One-and-Only Child!'

The Ravelling Man gave a snort of disdain. 'Call yourself what you please, mayfly. Your summer is ended, and winter is come.'

The little ones, too cold fully to understand what was happening, stood hugging each other for warmth. 'Can't we fly home now, Wendy? Somewhere warm?' Wendy nodded briskly and went from person to person rubbing handfuls of fairy dust into their hair.

Ravello watched her do it. When she was finished, he asked very sweetly: 'What? Without your shadows? An impossibility, I'm afraid, *stupidi bambini*. You may have fairy dust. You may have happy thoughts (though somehow I doubt it). But without a shadow *no one can fly*. Why do you suppose I took them?' Reaching into the sea chest, he lifted out their shadows, all neatly rolled up like window-blinds, stiff-brittle with the cold. The Twins moved towards him, hands outstretched. Teasingly he held the scrolls high above their heads.

'What, will you hold our own shadows to ransom?' demanded Pan.

'Faith no, blowfly. I hold nothing captive. I have a horror of confinement. Ask any of my animals. I shall free your shades to go their way!' Then Hook opened his good hand and let go the shadows—gave them into the teeth of the biting wind. The silhouettes of six children went dancing out over the abyss, tumbling and colliding and rolling themselves into a single, grubby ball. Each explorer felt a searing pain as each shadow tore into tatters on the gale.

'Hook, you are a scoundrel and a villain. Only the Devil steals a man's shadow!'

Ravello gave a dismissive wave of one sleeve. 'In the unlikely event you live long enough, they will re-grow. With every grief that befalls a man, his shadow increases. Have you not seen how I trail behind me a shadow like a leak from the Quink Ink factory? But then you have not heard my sad story, have you? Oh, you should, you should! I know how you children *love* your stories! So let me tell it. The story of Captain James Hook, yes? A man I was heartily fond of once, I confess it. A man with the strength and vitality to climb any mountain, to hunt down any treasure . . . Pay good heed.' And he began then and there to recount his life history.

'Once upon a time, Jas. Hook was a child. (How is it that children find that so hard to believe—that grown-ups were ever young?) He was a child just like you . . . *but better!* He excelled! Name any sport, and James Hook mastered it. On the playing fields of Eton College he could have writ his name large enough for the constellations to see from Outer Space! Let Latin go hang. Let mathematics sink. Let foreign languages remain a mystery. Hook was a sportsman! Winning was all in all to him. Let him but see his name on the sporting cups in Eton's trophy cabinet, and his heart would have filled with joy for ever! Just as you, Pan, gave up everything to be forever young, so I—acch!—*he*—*Hook*—gave up all to be the best, the fastest, the strongest, highest, fittest . . . By Skylights, but I kept a straight bat!'

The north wind hooted around the peak of Neverpeak. Whenever Ravello fell silent, the wind took over from him, bullying the children.

'But mothers are mothers. And mothers must pay their dressmakers before paying out for such trifles as *school fees*. So James Hook's dreams were ended by a vain rustle of taffeta. His mother came on Sports Day to fetch me— *him*—away from College. The other boys were competing for prizes which, in one more day, would have been his— for honours and laurels that would have . . .' He broke off, picturing the Headmaster's hand extended towards him, hearing the cheers of School House . . . His head rose; his shoulders squared. Then Disappointment struck again, like stomach cramp. 'Since Hook could not win 'em fair and square, he emptied the trophy cabinet and took every sporting prize away with him. His Treasure. His objects of desire.'

The Explorers gasped. 'You *stole your school cups?*'

Ravello took out a handkerchief speckled with acid burns and holes, and wiped his nose. 'Not good form, I admit, but if mothers will be mothers, then boys will be boys. Or pirates, in my case. Thus began James Hook's life of crime. On the journey home he made up his mind: he would cut loose from home and family, and come to Neverland—this one place in the world where a boy can shape his own destiny! He travelled by airship. Here, in this place, he crashed. In this place he left his Treasure and dragged his carcass down to the Lagoon and a life of greed and pillage. But his heart he left up here, meaning always to return one day and find it. So I would have! I would . . . *but for Pan!*

'That weevil in the meat. That fishbone in the gullet. That malaria in the bloodstream! First he took my right hand . . . *Hook's* hand, I mean—his bowling hand, his tiller hand, his rowing and fencing and . . . But let that pass. Then he consigned Hook to the belly of a crocodile! Ha! You think this mountain is a fearful place to die? You should taste life inside a saltwater crocodile! Lightless, airless tomb awash with digestive juices; a run-down clock wedged in the small of the back, and scarce room to turn over. What more terrible a grave! He lived on the eggs of the crocodile—a female. (Did you know she was a female?) Oh, how well acquainted Hook grew with the interior anatomy of the adult female saltwater crocodile!

'Each day the stomach acid burned him and the stench choked him . . . But I refused . . . *Hook refused* to take deadness. Gone were his days of playing the Good Sport; as he lay there and suffered his sea change, Hook thought on nothing but *revenge!*

'Then and there it started, unbidden, without him lifting a finger. For the bottle of poison he kept always in my breast pocket cracked and leaked and loosed its venom into the crocodile, into the Lagoon, into . . .' The sweeping gesture of his outstretched hook took in the whole wintry landscape that surrounded Neverpeak. 'At last, when the beast died of poisoning, he cut his way out with his hook—out of the creature's belly—and made him a pair of boots from the remnant. I would not—*dash it!*—*he* would not take deadness, you see!

'But the man who slithered into the daylight was not Hook. It was a digest of the man. Gone the scarlet coat, the britches, the glossy hair. The pride. They had dissolved all—flesh and hair and coat and colour and soul, in the bile of the crocodile. And sleep!—ah, agony!—the gift of sleep was gone! All that emerged was *this* . . . this SOFTNESS of a man! A thing like a sponge. A thing like a dead thing. From my panache to my underwear, all was frizzled to wool! The Hookness of Hook was eaten away and all that remained was Ravello, the Ravelling Man! Even my dear old ship presented herself to *you*, Pan, rather than to me! Try as I might, I could not summon her out of the Lagoon—could not *draw* her to me, for there was no magnetism left in me. The iron in my soul all rusted away, you see, as I lay in the briny slops of that crocodillo's belly!

'It was some comfort to find how the world, too, had *changed* during my imprisonment: how my little bottle of poison had worked its worst on Neverland; seeping through the Neverwood and the wetlands; cramping the summer months until the very year itself doubled up in pain!

'Not much was left of Hook, as I say, in this miserable *chinchilla* of a man. Only the dreary nag of longing. Only that oldest, deepest desire to recover his Treasure from the remote place he left it. And there was the biggest joke of all in this most hellish of Divine Comedies. *I . . . could . . . not . . . wish!* I could not wish any more than I could sleep. Only the iron will of James Hook could open that Treasure Chest there and find my . . . his . . . our . . . *dash and blight you!*—the Treasure that lay in there.

'See then how I found me an *understudy*. A proxy. A substitute. The only one in Neverland whose willpower equalled that of James Hook. Are you not grateful to me? Oh, what I would give to *look* like Hook again, to *swagger* like Hook, to blare and *terrify* like Hook! You should be grateful, Pan! Think how I drove you on, with thirst and flattery—how I bled the Pan out of you and replaced it with temper and tyranny. See how, with a coat and tie and boots, I turned you—scrubby boy that you are—from a mere child into the greatest pirate of them all—into Captain James Hook!'

'**NO!** *No*. No. I am Pan!' said Peter. 'I will always be young, and no one else in the whole world will *ever* be like me! And you, Hook, will always be my sworn enemy and I shan't rest until . . .'

'Tish. You are all fire and fury, lad.' Ravello flapped a

listless hand as if to be rid of a fly. 'Now that you have lost, you should cultivate patience. Like me. A spell inside a saltwater amphibian would pacify you; let me commend it to you . . . But no more rancour. Give me your hand. You have served your purpose, little Captain. I have what I came here for. Let us shake hands and be reconciled.' And he actually extended his good left hand in its overlong sleeve, to help Peter to his feet. Peter lashed out with his sword, but its saw-teeth simply snagged in the wool of the sleeve, and the hand within gripped his hand tighter than tight. 'So fierce! What would you have been, I wonder, if you had grown to manhood; if you had not opted for everlasting childhood. Would you have been a pirate like me?'

'Never!'

'No? A pilot, then. Or an actor, taking ten curtain calls to the applause of your adoring fans! A man of rank, I don't doubt it! A hero . . . Oh, but wait! I know! Of course! An *explorer*! A discoverer of new lands, writing your name in letters of gold on maps of the thirteen continents!'

Within Peter's hand the oily strands of wool began to separate, to unravel, to unknit. The numbing cold, the dizzying snow-flurries, the words Ravello sprinkled like salt over him, slowed Peter's thinking. The words had pictures attached to them, like little fluttering gift tags, and he really could almost see what life would be like if he were . . .

'What, then, what?' Hook badgered him, grinning—all the time grinning. 'Not an explorer. Something easier? Something not so taxing?'

Peter bridled. Did Ravello think he was not up to being an explorer? Absurd! Why, Peter could almost imagine . . .

'Don't answer him!'

A figure stumbled up on to the peak—a young man no one recognized—until they saw the tails of his evening shirt fluttering beneath his outgrown coat.

'Slightly!'

'Don't answer him, Peter!' called Slightly pointing his clarinet at the Ravelling Man.

Wendy ran to Slightly's side. His bigness made her feel awkward, but she could not help flinging her arms around him. 'Oh, you aren't a Roarer after all! You followed us! How cold your poor knees must be! I do wish I had made your coat bigger!'

'Don't answer him, Peter!' said Slightly again, never once taking his eyes off Ravello. 'He asked me the selfsame thing—*What do you want to be when you grow up?*—and the wool unravelled in my hand, and in that moment—in that moment, I started to grow. I have worked it out, you see, Ravelling Man!'

Ravello gave his strange, underwater laugh, though his vexation was plain. 'Slightly-wiser now, I see.'

Peter Pan looked up at Hook, incredulous. 'You would

have made me grow up? Under cover of a handshake!'

Hook met the accusation with a jaunty shrug. 'Not I. You yourself. The moment a child answers the question, *"What do you want to be when you grow up?"* he is halfway to being an adult. He has betrayed childhood and Looked Ahead. He has joined the ranks of those clerks and chicken-pluckers and box-packers who scan the Situations Vacant column in the newspapers.' His grip on Peter's hand tightened and he hauled the whole boy up to a level with his face. It was a terrible face, scarred by grief, regret, stomach-acid, and loathing. 'Say that you *did* think ahead when I asked you! Tell me you pictured yourself a grown man, rowing your canoe up the Amazon River—or dragging your sled over pack-ice towards True South! Curse you, Slightly! One moment more and I would have done what no mother or father could do: I would have stolen childhood away from the boy Pan!'

Still Slightly pointed an accusing finger at Hook. Still he raged: 'That man told the Roarers you poisoned them, Peter, and made them grow older, but I say it was him! I say *he* poisoned them!'

'He poisoned all Neverland!' snarled Peter. His face was so close to the pirate's that their noses touched. 'I should carve you to the bone, villain!'

'You would find nothing there but my hatred of thee, Peter Pan,' said Ravello and threw him to the ground.

All this while, the Twins had been trotting to and fro with twigs from the treasure chest, to make a bonfire. As often as they piled up two armfuls of fuel, the wind scattered them again. (The blizzard grew worse with every passing moment, lashing the mountain peak with flails of snow.) Slightly went to their rescue, pinning the wood in place with bags of gold and bolts of silk from among the Treasure.

'Oh, I'm so glad you didn't turn brigand, Slightly!' said First Twin with a sniff.

'Or forget all about us, Slightly!' said the Second.

But what else could Slightly have done, knowing the danger they were in? What choice did he have but to dog their footsteps all the way to the Point of No Return? Slightly was adult now, and though growing up is a blight and a nuisance, grown-ups do have one great merit: they cannot help caring and going on caring.

So Slightly helped the Twins to build the bonfire which might just save his friends from an icy death on the summit of Neverpeak. John ran to the sea chest to fetch a match, but Ravello slammed its lid shut with the toe of his boot and gave it a push, so that it rolled to the very brink.

'Give me a match, pirate,' John demanded.

'Don't speak to him!' snapped Peter. 'I have banished him to Nowhereland and nobody must speak to him. I will light the fire, as I always lit fires in the grate at the Wendy

House! By Imagination!' But though he strained and struggled, though he banged his head on the ground and wrenched at his glossy hair with desperate fingers, Peter could no more conjure up fire than he could imagine them their supper. Ravello had combed the Imagination out through the ends of his hair, you see.

The Twins were sure they could do it. After all, hadn't they set the Neverwood alight to kill the timber dragon? But Ravello laughed his mirthless laugh. 'Ha! Do you really credit yourselves with that, *doppel-kinder*? It was *I* who torched the Neverwood! Turned loose my animals. Sacked my circus-hands (Roarers, every one). Set fire to my beautiful tent . . . Burned my bridges. For as soon as I saw the Wendy girl, I knew my waiting was over. The time had come for revenge. What is a circus in comparison with *sweet revenge?*'

The air was crammed with snowflakes—as though a goose-feather pillow had burst. Without the red frock coat, Peter was gibbering with cold and he struggled to pull the white tie from round his throat.

'A match, Ravello. Let us get this fire lit and talk after!' called Curly.

'A match, Ravello. Quickly!' said Tootles. 'Aren't you cold too?'

'What's the little word that gets things done?' said the Ravelling Man, his voice high and mocking.

Then the Explorers wanted to send him to Nowhereland and never have to speak to him again.

'Please,' said Wendy coldly.

'Please,' said Curly.

'Please,' said John.

Ravello gave a tug on the rope, and brought the wheeled sea chest back to his feet like a chastened pet. He opened its lid and took out a box of lucifers, shaking it gently: a sound like a baby's rattle. Only one match left. 'Tell me again. What's the little word?'

'Please!' said Tootles.

'Please!' chorused the Twins.

('Ah! Now I see!' said Peter to himself, puzzle solved.)

'*PLEASE!*' said all but Peter.

'WRONG,' said Ravello, striking the match against the stubble of his unshaven jaw. The flare lit up his face. It was a wretched face, scarred by his time inside the crocodile, scarred by time passing where no time should have passed. Only the aristocratic tilt of his head and the fire in his bleached-brown eyes proved that Pan's deadliest foe, Captain James Hook, was still living within. 'Let me think now. What *is* that little word that gets things done? Ah yes. Now I remember . . .'

Then he blew out the match and said, '*DIE!*'

CHAPTER NINETEEN
Burned

Wind smashed against the mountain. The scarlet treasure chest, still half-buried in snow, only banged its lid open and shut, open and shut. But the battered old sea trunk Ravello had pulled over such a distance on its springy wheels—*that* the wind shook and rocked and set rolling like a runaway perambulator. It rolled over the brink, arcing out into space and falling, falling, spilling out salt cellars, crockery, maps, tools, and string. They never heard it land; the blizzard was on them now, larding them with ice, filling their ears and eyes and hands with snow.

'Now you will die too, Hook!' cried Peter Pan.

The circus-pirate shrugged. 'I may. It is of no consequence. I have done what I set out to do. I have my Treasure. What else remains?'

'And has it made you happy, your "Treasure"?' asked Wendy crisply (because mothers always point out how badness doesn't bring joy, crime doesn't pay, thieves don't prosper).

Pained confusion disturbed Ravello's scarred face. 'How would I know?' he asked, taking out the Marathon Cup and gently caressing the inscription of his name now magically there on the base. 'Happiness is not a food I have tasted before. I do have a curious feeling inside me akin to chocolate cake. And fireworks. And the music of Mr Elgar.' That sounded suspiciously like Happiness to Wendy, but she did not say so, for fear it encouraged Hook in his wickedness.

John was busy rubbing two sticks together to try and make a spark. But even the sticks were shivering with cold. Curly was trying to build an igloo out of snow, where they could shelter until the blizzard passed. But igloos are not made of loose snow. Tootles said they should sing, to keep up their spirits, because that is what heroes do when things look blackest. And Ravello gave the strangest laugh and began the singing himself:

'*Jolly boating weather,*
And a hay harvest breeze,
Blade on the feather,
Shade off the trees . . .'

It was an Eton song. Peter—though he did not want to be an Eton boy, did not *want* to know the words—could not resist singing. So he sang as if he was firing cannon at the pirate, and every word might hole him.

'*Rugby may be more clever,*
Harrow may make more row,
But we'll row for ever,
Steady from stroke to bow . . .'

The blizzard pulled hair out of their heads. It ripped the seams of their blanket-coats. It kicked the snow in their faces and sent avalanches crashing down the mountain. The spit froze in their mouths. The words of the song rattled in their mouths like ice cubes. If they had not all linked arms and clung to each other, the wind would have thrown them off Neverpeak and tossed them into the sky.

'*And nothing in life shall sever,*
The chain that is round us now.

And nothing in life shall sever,
The chain that is round us now.'

If you suppose that Tinker Bell came to the rescue, I must tell you now you are wrong. Wishing had brought Tinker Bell back from a place far beyond Strange, and her wings were still sticky with improbability. Tinker Bell had nestled down to sleep again in the scarlet treasure chest. *Too cold,* she said drowsily. *Too noisy.'*

'. . . *And youth will be still in our faces,*
When we cheer for an Eton crew.
And youth will be still in our faces,
When . . .'

The words trailed away into the great silence that was waiting for them. Winter had gripped Neverpeak in its teeth and was shaking them to death.

Suddenly, like a wasp aiming for a picnic, something whirled past the Explorers that was not a snowflake. Glowing like a cinder it settled on the hasp of the treasure chest.

'FIREFLYER!'

In Neverland a treasure chest contains the treasure-seeker's dearest wish, and, unknown to anyone, it was *Fireflyer* who had wished for Tinker Bell.

Burned

Ever since that first intriguing mention—'*Do you know Tinker Bell?*'—the idea of her had been growing in Fireflyer's head, glowing in the dark little seedcase of his fairy skull. Everything he heard about her made him want to know more. He had plagued Slightly with questions and come to the conclusion that Tinker Bell—willing to drink poison and able to tell lies as big as albatrosses—was far too marvellous to be dead. Now, seeing Tinker Bell, his sugar coating of fairy dust glowed with the heat of Love-at-First-Sight. It melted the varnish on the chest.

Tinker Bell opened her eyes, but seemed to think she was dreaming Fireflyer, because she gave only an apologetic little smile and said, '*So cold. Too cold. Got to go now.*' And then the snow rampaged between them like an army of jealous fairies.

'*Fairies die if other fairies ignore them,*' Fireflyer complained, but she took no notice. After a moment or two more Fireflyer announced grandly: '*I'm not going to light any old bonfire. I WON'T DO IT. I REFUSE. I WON'T!*'

(Well, you have to remember: the thing he did best was lying.) Then he plunged like a drop of molten gold into the woodpile.

'Oh, Fireflyer, no!' cried Wendy.

'You will burn yourself all up!' cried Tootles.

'Oh, my dear idiot!' cried Slightly.

Under its blanket of snow, the bonfire sagged and settled. It seemed impossible that anything could make it burn now. But Fireflyer did. Gradually the twigs turned from white to brown, then from brown to orange, and with a crackling cackle, flames came to life, fanned by the howling wind into a blazing beacon-fire. Fireflyer's body-heat had lit the bonfire, and Neverpeak was topped by a triumphal flame visible from all over the island.

Some of the flames burned with the same colour as Fireflyer. Some of the ash that flew upwards looked like small charred wings. The Company turned their faces away, covered their eyes sooner than see what befell the brave little fairy . . . all except Peter. He went so close that he was haloed round with flame and his eyebrows singed; and he bent and peered and called and reached in his swordfish sword in case he could rescue Fireflyer from a fiery end. The sword crumbled into shards in the heat.

'Be careful, Peter!' cried Wendy as cinders spilled out over his feet.

'I swore I would stick by you all the way!' he answered. 'But oh, what a fairy!'

'What a whopping liar!' John agreed, in awe.

'Like Tink in the old days!' said Curly.

Then Tinker Bell well and truly woke up. Something exciting was going on. Lives hung in the balance. People were remembering her fondly. Also, another fairy was getting all the attention. That was quite enough to do the trick. *'Wait, young man!'*

Tinker Bell darted towards the fire, meaning to follow Fireflyer, but her movements were still sleep-slurred and Peter's hand whipped out and caught her and kept tight hold. 'Enough lost for one day,' he said gruffly.

It is odd, because there were never very many twigs and turfs and grasses to begin with. What with Hook's Treasure, dog bones, silk, sago, and gold, the Twins had had very little fuel to work with. Their bonfire was only small. And yet that fire burned bigger and brighter than any beacon on the night of the Armada. Magic fuel must be more combustible.

They were able to cook the bread dough and spaghetti, melt snow and make a gallon of tea. They sent smoke signals summoning help (though the blizzard did its best to smudge them out). Finally, the smoke scarfed up the snowflakes and carried them off. The mountain felt warmth at its peak and remembered its childhood. (It had been a volcano once, remember.) Perhaps the mountain (unlike Peter or Hook) had only happy memories of youth, because remembering made it smile.

Oh, I know it is unusual—it may never have happened before or since—but the mountain smiled; no other word for it. All its downs turned up. It flexed the muscles of its four faces—north, south, east, and west—and the glaciers cracked and the ice bridges fell and the snow could not keep its grip. Trees emerged, astonished, and shook the snow out of their hair. Grass grew through, stubbly at first, then shaggy like a full beard. Waterfalls unfroze with a splashing rush and startled flowers into opening.

On the top of Neverpeak, hunter and prey, villain and hero, child, adult, and fairy stood in a circle, overlapping at hand or knee or wing, eyeing each other like animals at a waterhole. They watched the blizzard blow away into the distance and out to sea, soon no bigger than Wendy's apron blown off the washing-line. The fire went out at last.

'I must go and look for the silly chap, I suppose,' said Tinker Bell in a world-weary sigh (though her wings were throbbing in a dozen excitable colours). And wriggling free of Peter's hand, she darted straight into the smoking bonfire and instantly disappeared with a fizz and a crackle. Two small fairies do not make much of a glow, but the air seemed darker without them.

'We must fight, you and I,' said Peter to the Ravelling Man.

'What with?' sneered Ravello, turning away. 'Name your non-existent weapon. Besides, we are both Oppidans—Eton boys. Bad form to scrap, particularly in front of the ladies.' And touching his frizzled hairline in salute to Wendy and Tootles, he moved away with a happy skip of his crocodile boots.

Peter pounced after him—*'Let's finish it here and now,*

you coward!'—and felt a steel hook brush his cheek as Ravello turned and held him at bay.

'Do you really think the choice is yours, moth?' hissed Ravello. 'Did you never play a game called "Consequences"?' Snatching the tattered treasure map from Peter, he pretended to write, with his hook in place of a quill pen.

'Once upon a time there was:	A boy called Pan.
In a place called:	Neverland
Who met a	pirate named Jas. Hook
And they	fought to the death.
And the Consequence was . . .'	

'That James Hook got fed to a crocodile!' Peter broke in triumphantly.

'Ah yes!' countered Hook. 'But every consequence has further consequences, my boy! Everything you do comes back to haunt you: each enemy you feed to a crocodile— every boy you turn away. Do you seriously think you will ever see the Neverwood again, now that I have plucked the wings off you? You put me in my coffin once: in my crocodile coffin. Do you seriously think you can kill a man who has risen from the dead? Read your history books . . . ah! But I was forgetting: you cannot read, can you, *ignoramus minimus*? I must tell you, then: it is no great feat for explorers to reach their goal. It is the *homeward* journey that finishes them. The broken clock is ticking. Prepare to face the consequences of your past deeds! I have no need to kill you, cock-a-doodle: *that task I will leave to Neverland!'*

CHAPTER TWENTY
Ill Luck

The bonfire was a black heap of charcoal. The Twins pulled out two sticks and drew a picture of Ravello on the rock, and threw stones at it. Wendy, who had been watching Peter's face since the pirate left, pulled out another piece and wrote in big letters across the highest jutting pinnacle of rock:

Pan's Peak

'Well?' she said, standing back proudly, wiping clean her hands on her pirate-flag dress.

'What?' said Peter blankly, not able to read it. So

Wendy drew a cockerel with its beak open, shrieking

'Cock-a-doodle-doo!'

and Peter understood and smiled. It was a small smile, a
worn-out smile. His fingers were still hooked through the
white Eton tie that circled his neck like a hangman's noose.

John, wanting to draw a picture of his own on the rock,
pulled another blackened twig out of the bonfire . . . and
found a fairy sitting on its tip, sooty from head to foot!
An ink-blot of a fairy.

'Fireflyer! You're alive!'

Naturally, said the ink-blot. They crowded eagerly round,
and Tootles made a little bath out of a cup of cool tea.

But as the fairy sank from sight, turning the tea black with
soot, another voice behind them said, *Don't believe a word he says. He
is such a liar, that boy!* And a similarly filthy Tinker Bell clambered
out of the bonfire and roughly hauled Fireflyer out of the
teacup. *Ladies first,* she said, and got in. They all had to close
their eyes while she washed the soot off.

'So fairies are fireproof,' said John, who had a scientist's
curiosity about these things.

Only on Wednesdays, said Fireflyer categorically.

'I think it's Friday,' said Curly.

Oh dear. Then I must be dead, said Fireflyer.

After that Tinker Bell and Fireflyer would only speak to
each other, because they were so much in love. They did

not seem to hear anything that was said to them; took no interest in the gathering up of litter and treasure, the raising of the rainbow banner, the scanning of the island through Hook's brass telescope.

'Come, then, if you are coming!' called Peter. But the fairies ignored him.

'People die if fairies ignore them!' said Slightly teasingly. But the two fairy lovers only leapt into the treasure chest and pulled shut the lid with a deafening slam. When Curly opened it again, there was nothing and no one inside. Not even any cold sago pudding.

Going Down should have been easy. The cold was not so fierce. The mountain was not so slippery. Lower down, the air was not so thin. Here and there they found wreckage from the sea chest: a pram wheel, a pair of sugar tongs, an empty matchbox. And yet with each slope and cliff-face and danger they overcame, Peter grew paler and slower and wearier. He wrenched at the Eton cravat until his neck was a livid red. He tripped and stumbled and fell, and each time took longer to get back on his feet.

'Let's pitch camp here, Captain,' said Slightly when they reached a grassy ledge, but found he was still banished and in Nowhereland, because Peter would not speak to him. The others sat down then and there, exhausted, but

Peter pressed on, head down, shoulders rounded, hands pressed to his ribcage.

'I don't go about with grown-ups,' he muttered. 'Grown-ups can't be trusted.' But the voice was more defeated than defiant. Then he leaned against the cliff and coughed and coughed until his legs pleated under him, coughed and coughed until he was kneeling on the ground, coughed and coughed until his forehead was on the grass, coughed and coughed until he slumped over sideways . . . and disappeared entirely over the brink of the ledge.

Further down the mountain, Captain Jas. Hook—or Ravello if you prefer—sat with his long legs encircling a bird's nest, holing one egg at a time with his hook and sucking out the contents. For the first time in his life, he was finding it hard not to whistle for sheer joy (though everyone knows whistling is damnably unlucky).

He picked a blade of grass, and pinning it between two fingers of his good hand blew a single quacking note. Eddies of movement stirred the bracken on the plain below him. Ravello smiled to see it.

Then, unannounced, a boy came slithering down the escarpment behind him and all but dislodged him from his perch. Thinking he was under attack, Hook jumped to his feet, a bird's egg still impaled on his hook. But the boy only jack-knifed around his ankles and lay like a dead thing, eyelids half open.

Before Hook had a chance to recognize Peter and raise a hook to impale him like an eggshell, lots more children came sliding down the cliff, showering him with earth and pebbles, and all yelling like dervishes. '*Leave him be!*'

'*Let him go!*'

'*Don't touch him!*'

'*He must not be touched!*'

'I'll nurse you, Peter!' cried Tootles and ran to Peter's side. 'I'll take care of you!'

John rushed at Hook, sword drawn. 'This is your doing, you blaggard!'

'I—' the pirate began, too startled for retaliation or glee.

The Explorers sank to their knees round their Leader. 'Maybe he has new-moanier,' Tootles said, 'from wearing only his shirt in the blizzard.'

Tootles tried to cover Peter over with the scarlet frock coat, but Wendy gave a cry of horror and ran and pulled it off again, throwing it at Hook. 'You've killed him, haven't you!' she yelled.

'I?' said Hook.

Tootles felt his forehead, looked for a pulse, stroked his hair, and laid her head on his chest to listen for a heartbeat. Then she sat back with a sob, and declared . . .

'Peter is Dead!'

A quiver went through Neverland then that made the horizon buckle and the reflections climb out of every pool and lake and lagoon. The League of Pan covered him with the rainbow banner. In the dreadful silence that followed, the accusations stirred again.

'He died of getting so cold,' said Second Twin.

'Sooner than be like you!' said John, and jabbed the tip of the swordfish blade in Hook's face.

'No! It was that tie round his throat. It choked the life out of him!' said Wendy.

'*Your* tie!' snarled John and jabbed the blade-tip at Hook's woolly throat.

'Or else you made him think what he would be when he grew up, and it broke his heart!' said Slightly.

'All down to *you*,' said John, jabbing Hook in the chest.

'Or maybe he hated being Hook so much that he upped and died on purpose!' suggested First Twin.

'Happy now?' said John and jabbed Hook in the belt buckle.

'Or maybe Hook poisoned him with the salt,' said Curly, 'or the comb or the boot polish or the tea or the berries or . . . or . . .'

'. . . like he poisoned all Neverland!' growled John.

Hook smartly side-stepped to avoid John's next sword thrust. 'He is not yet dead, you fools,' he said between gritted teeth, and pointed at the small body on the ground.

The ripple was no bigger than the surface of a river when a pike swims by, but the rainbow banner did ripple from some movement beneath it.

'No thanks to you!' said John and jabbed again.

Hook gave an exasperated gasp, stamped on the blade with one crocodile-skin boot and snapped it in twelve places. 'I did not *poison* him or *strangle* him or *cozen* him out of his life!' said Hook, writhing with irritation. 'Did I not preserve him through danger and hardship? Did I not pluck him from certain death at the ice-bridge? Not out of fondest affection, I confess, but I did so. Do you not understand? I *needed* the brat! For my grand plan! Make him ill? I was relying on him to recover my Treasure! He was more Hook than I am: do you think I would have poisoned my own likeness? Were you not there when I abandoned you to the mercies of the Island? When I left it for land and weather to kill you all? If ever I raise a hand to finish Peter Pan it will be this hand!'

And he brandished his hook, first in John's face and then over the boy Pan. When he aimed a downward slash at Peter's throat, the children screamed, thinking they were witnessing cold-blooded murder, and Slightly called Hook 'a coward and a monster'. But the hook caught only the fabric of the white tie round Peter's neck and hauled the boy within reach of Hook's good hand.

In the time it takes to click two fingers, the white knot

was untied and Peter fell back, cracking his head on the ground but otherwise unmurdered. 'Now are you satisfied, madam?' said Hook to Wendy, and slumped down again, his back to the group.

Tootles knelt and whispered in Peter's ear. 'Are we playing doctors and nurses, Peter? Oh, please say we are! I'm your nurse and you're the patient and you have to get better and be everso thankful.' But the boy on the ground did not stir. When she trickled pretend medicine in at his lips, it trickled out again at the corner of his mouth. His skin was clammy and the breath rasped in his throat. Tootles whispered, 'You're not playing this game right, Peter. Really you're not.'

First Twin bundled up the discarded red coat and hugged it to him, as if it were Peter himself.

Thus the band of Explorers formed a circle once more, on the slopes of Neverpeak, not blasted this time by wind and snow but by the terrible possibility that the boy on the ground was dying, might still die, and they had no idea why, or how to prevent it.

There were two moons that night. Alongside the midnight moon, dark-eyed with worry, hung her quavering reflection, risen from the sea in need of comforting company. Their two anxious white faces gazed down at the slopes of Neverpeak, offering bandages of moonbeam.

CHAPTER TWENTY-ONE
Coming of Age

Remembering Peter's words, they sent Hook to Nowhereland, refusing to speak a word to him, pretending he no longer existed. But there he remained, bunched up on himself, eyes glimmering in the dark, wide awake as usual. Was it to witness the death of his sworn enemy, or because it was too dark to descend the mountain, or simply because he liked to be contrary?

'Go away,' John said. 'You have been banished. It's in the rules. You have to go.'

'Whose rules?' said Hook. 'Go yourselves. I was here first.'

'What, are you waiting for Peter to die?' said Wendy.

'Might be.'

'Only a bad sport breaks the rules,' John brooded sulkily, and vowed not to speak another word to the man—until a question entered his head that wanted answering. '. . . Anyway, I don't believe what you said. I thought you were a pirate before you came here, not a schoolboy. "Bosun to Blackbeard: blood-thirstiest pirate ever to sail the seven seas." That's what I heard!'

'Huh! Lies. A slur put about by my enemies. I have never served *under* any man! Why would Hook serve a styleless ship's rat who could not count past five. I doubt Blackbeard could *spell* Eton, let alone wear the old school tie. I would not have suffered him aboard a ship of mine to chip paint.'

'And where are your scurvy pirate cronies now?' asked John, trying to sound haughty and disdainful, though secretly he just wanted to know. (John would have liked to be a pirate but for the robbing and killing part of it.)

'I sent them off to do their bit in the War,' said Hook. 'As every man should. They sent me postcards first off. From Belgium and France. Then they forgot, I suppose. The postcards stopped. I imagine they were having too good a time. I imagine they were too busy living it up on booty and the spoils of war. Spending their loot on cake and beautiful

French women. Unwilling to return to the drudgery of life aboard the *Jolly Roger.*'

Wendy nodded. 'I like to imagine that as well,' she said, 'every time I think about my brother Michael.' Their eyes met for the briefest of moments, during which they understood each other perfectly.

'I see *you* didn't go to the War, though,' said John sarcastically.

The pirate glared at him murderously and said in a roaring whisper as low and cold as a subterranean river, 'Thanks to that one there, I was *UNFIT FOR DUTY*!'

'Hush!' said Nurse Tootles in a flutter of fright. 'We should let Peter sleep. Sleep is good for people. Sleep does wonders.'

Hook, who had not slept for twenty years, gave a low and bitter laugh and turned his back on them, hunching his wool around him.

Suddenly Curly was up on his feet. 'What Peter needs is a doctor!' he declared desperately. 'A real doctor!'

Everyone looked out from their mountain perch at the wilderness waste and wild vastnesses of Neverland and wondered how a doctor was to be conjured from such shaggy chaos. Doctors are spawned in ponds of antiseptic and on plains of clean linoleum or starched sheets. Neverland is not their natural habitat. And yet Curly already knew where one was to be found; it showed in the set of his jaw. Taking one deep breath, he crossed to where the pirate sat slumped under his fleece. 'Ask me,' he said, sinking the fingers of both hands in Ravello's sleeve. 'Ask me now.'

Slightly sprang up. 'No, Curly, don't!'

'Ask me, Ravello.'

There was a mooing confusion of worry and questions from the others who did not understand. Hook scowled at Curly and tried to ease himself free, but Curly hung on, fierce as a terrier. 'Ask me, Hook. Ask me what I want to be when I grow up.'

'But, Curly!' protested Slightly, trying to pull him away. 'Think what you are doing! Do you want to be like me— grown-up like me? Never able to go home? There's nothing left for me but to be a Roarer. Do you want to be a Roarer, Curly?'

Curly swallowed hard and began to tug on the tangle of greasy wool that was both sleeve and arm of the pirate. Ravello's face contorted with pain, and he said, 'Listen to your friend, Master Curly. If the cock-a-doodle lives, do you really think he will thank you? He will turn you out, as he turned out all the rest. He won't suffer grown-ups in his Company.' The man's eyes were liquid with midnight, and where there should have been stars reflected in them there were flying sparks and shards of eggshell. 'The brat is dying, Mr Curly. Nothing can save Pan now. Ah, but who am I to dissuade you from your chosen fate? So tell me, Master Curly: what do you want to be when you—'

'*A doctor!*' Curly interrupted, sinking in his fingers almost to the bone of Hook's arm. So steeped was the fabric in poison that it cancelled out the youthful magic of Neverland and let Time soak in through the pores of Curly's tender skin. As his fists filled up with unravelling wool, he felt the squibs and sparklers fizzle out in his head, to be replaced with the dull gleam of good sense and cleverness. His nose could smell chloroform and liniment. White coats paraded through his imagination like starched ghosts. His pockets rattled with hypodermics, thermometers, and spatulas. Curly wished so hard to be a doctor that he grew taller, then and there, sloughing his blanket coat and even his wealth of curly hair. The growing pains were fearsome, but he kept tight hold of Ravello.

And the bigger he grew the more he remembered of being a doctor—after all, he had been one before—back in Fotheringdene, before the quest to Neverpeak. He remembered his studies now, at medicine school, his days in Fotheringdene County Hospital. And all this while his hands filled with the wool that was both Ravello's arm and Ravello's clothing. He laid bare the steel hook and the scars inflicted by the crocodile. Ravello rose to his feet with a bloodcurdling yell, but found himself no taller than Doctor Curly Darling MD, MRCS.

Peter Pan in Scarlet

'I'm sorry if I hurt you, sir,' said Curly (now that he was a doctor, he regretted causing pain to anyone) and emptied his hands of the crinkled wool, which spilled to the ground around the pirate's crocodile-skin boots. Instinctively the children moved away from Curly. (Doctors are almost as scary as pirates, what with their cold hands and dangerous handwriting. And they only ever visit when you are feeling too ill to make friends.)

Pulling a stethoscope from his pocket, Doctor Curly knelt down beside Peter and listened to the fluttering beat of his heart. It was the sound of Fairyland at war with itself. It was the sound of Eternal Youth dying, dying, dying.

But he clearly heard something else as well. Breaking the tip off his own swordfish blade (how small it seemed now in his big, cold hands) Curly cut a hole just over Peter's heart and, using the sugar tongs, drew out a length of something grey and wispy and flecked with soot. 'I think that this may be the source of the trouble,' he said.

Back in the house in Cadogan Square, in sneezing the last sneeze of her cold, Wendy had reached out for a handkerchief and tucked it into her sleeve—a grown woman's handkerchief tucked into the sleeve of a girl's sundress. And inside that handkerchief, unknown to her, *a strand of London fog!*

220

Coming of Age

In the Neverwood, when Peter had mopped the blood from his face using her handkerchief, he had breathed in that same strand, and it had wound itself about his heart, tightening its grip day by day.

Not the burning of the Neverwood, nor shipwreck, nor the touch of witches, nor the crushing weight of hostile fairies had got the better of Peter Pan; not hunger nor cold; not Ravello's salt, nor his words of temptation were killing Peter; not even Hook's little bottle of poison—which had blighted all Neverland—had brought Peter Pan to the edge of death. Only a strand of London fog.

Dr Curly made hard work of getting to his feet, as only grown-ups can. 'Come, Slightly. Time for us to go,' he said. And cutting his own door in the air with his surgeon's lancet, he stepped through it and into banishment.

'Where are you going?' said Hook, still clutching an arm unravelled to the bone.

'I broke the Rule and grew,' said Curly peaceably. 'And *unlike some people*, I know how to play by the Rules. I prescribe sleep for that arm, Ravello. As Nurse Tootles says, Sleep is a great healer. Sleep and Time.' And with that he left, drawing Slightly away, skidding noisily and clumsily down the mountainside by the light of two moons.

With a deep sigh and then with a deeper intake of breath,

Peter Pan sat up. Putting one small hand to his chest, he felt the life pouncing through his bloodstream, put back his head and crowed:

'Cock-a-doodle-doo!'

Peter Pan restored to health was a wonderful sight. He could turn cartwheels, walk on his hands, and leap from ledge to ledge as nimbly as a mountain goat. In fact (being no longer a pirate or superstitious about whistling) he whistled up all the chamois goats that lived locally, and mounted his friends on their backs, so that they fairly cantered down the slopes and precipices of Neverpeak towards the dismal plain below. Even Humpty Dumpty jumping off his wall never had so much fun. Ravello was left far behind, maimed, unthought-of, and as slow-moving as a sloth by comparison with the League of Pan.

Nobody would have mistaken Peter for any dandified pirate captain now. The glossy ringlets Ravello had combed into place were soon tangled and matted, and stood up in wild confusion, lightening in the sunshine. Butterflies clamoured round the bright colours of his tunic and on their wings brought pollen that made him sneeze.

'Every time I sneeze,' he bragged, 'astrologers in China spot a new planet coloured like a soap bubble!' He went to blow his nose, and when Wendy snatched the handkerchief out of his hand, simply laughed and wiped his nose on his shirtsleeve instead. Then he made up a rude song about baboons, and they sang it at the top of their voices all the way down to the monkey-puzzle trees.

Not Wendy, though. She did not sing. She clutched the handkerchief between her two hands and began to weep inconsolably. The others stopped singing—'**bumti-boo-ba-boo-oo-boons!**'—to stare at her. 'It was all my fault!' she wailed. 'I might have killed Peter, and all for a silly sneeze!'

But Peter did not trouble with 'what-ifs' or 'might-have-beens'. He did not even mind about having no treasure to show for the quest to Neverpeak; the hunt for treasure is always more fun than the finding of it. After all, what could he have wished for, having what he had already: friends and freedom and adventure and youth? Wendy, though, washed out the handkerchief in a little stream of icy water from the melting glacier (for fear any fog remained), then pinned it to her coat to dry.

And because it had belonged once to a grown-up Wendy Darling, she began to remember things. She remembered Cadogan Square and a little girl called Jane, remembered grocery bills and washdays, committee work and a husband, appointments at the dentist, and putting the bins out on Tuesdays. Just as dreams of Neverland had disturbed her peace of mind while she was in London, so dreams of home began to hover around her now, as the butterflies hovered around Peter.

Butterflies and wasps!

Climbing down the monkey-puzzle trees was no more pleasant than before. The insects stung, the sap stuck their fingers and knees together, the spines pricked, and the twigs broke under their weight. Suddenly, to the sound of banshee wailing and hooting and shrieking and yelling, the trees began to toss and flex and lash about, sending wasp's nests and pinecones tumbling. The children clung on for as long as they could, then Peter sprang rashly out into empty air and everyone else lost their grip and dropped through the trees.

The lower branches showed no interest in catching them—only the nets stretched wide by the Roarers who had been lying in ambush for days.

CHAPTER TWENTY-TWO
Consequences

They had him at last, all those boys who had broken the Rule and grown bigger; all those boys Peter had banished to Nowhereland, and who hated him for it, with a deadly venom.

The Roarers bound their prisoners to the trunks of the monkey-puzzle trees and spent the morning throwing pine cones at them for the fun of it. Meanwhile, they discussed what they would do with Peter Pan; how they would put him to death.

'Hang him!'

'No rope.'

'Shoot him!'

'No gun.'

'Cut off his head, then!'

'Or bury 'im alive.'

'Hit him with a rock.'

'Or cut out his lights.'

'Whatever you do, don't throw me into a briar patch!' said Peter with a glimmer of a smile. Wendy had once told him the story of Brer Rabbit and how he tricked his way out of just such trouble.

But the Roarers were not fooled. They too knew the story of Brer Rabbit: they had heard it from Peter as they sat at his feet, happy little Lost Boys all.

'Make him walk the plank!' suggested the Twins, thinking the Roarers might forget they were on dry land and not aboard ship, and would think that Peter had drowned.

But the Roarers were not fooled.

'Scare him to death!' said John, knowing that Peter was far too brave for that to work.

But the Roarers were not fooled.

'Let us go, and I will be a mother to you all,' said Wendy. That was not a trick. It was an honest and straightforward offer made out of the goodness of her heart. But, amazingly, the Roarers did not want a mother. Full as they were of rage and disappointment, they believed mothers were almost as bad as Peter Pan.

Consequences

'Bog'll do it,' said the oldest, and the rest agreed.

'Nowt left after bogging.'

'Swamp the lot.' All the words in the world would not soften this sentence of death: the Roarers were going to drop Peter and his friends into quicksand.

'We demand a trial!' said Tootles (who had once been a high court judge, remember). But she found herself now in a place without justice or fair play. The Roarers had armed themselves with branches ripped from the corkscrew-dogwoods and dogwood-corktrees; now they drove the children towards their place of execution.

Not far to go. On each side of the spongy track, swamp softly sucked and seethed: a carpet of crimson moss unrolled to welcome the unwary and the doomed. The heights of Neverpeak still loomed over them, cutting out the eastern sky. The Roarers robbed the children of anything in their pockets, scrunched up the rainbow banner inside a grubby fist, then goaded everyone towards the red swamp.

'Give me a sword and I will fight you all single-handed!' declared Peter. 'Or are you too cowardly?'

But there was no appealing to the Roarers' valour or pride. Any notion of nobility had died on the day of their banishment. Graceful boyhood had deserted them, through no fault of their own, and left them burly and bumbling and bony; why should they give a hoot for honour or fair play? They jabbed their prisoners in the back, forcing them towards the quagmire.

'Who's first?' said the thinnest one, as they reached the brink.

'I am,' said Peter. 'Always.' And he thrust out his chest and tilted back his head and took one long, long stride out on to the quicksand. After his illness, he was so light that his weight barely dented the surface. 'You are supposed to grant me one last wish,' he said, turning to face his assassins. 'I ask that you free my friends. They never did you any wrong.'

The Roarers shrugged their bony shoulders up around their juggy ears. 'Any friend of yours . . .' said the articulate one, without bothering to finish the sentence. 'And we don't do wishes. Wishes is for fairies.'

The jellified ground sucked thoughtfully at Peter's little bare feet, decided it liked the taste, and closed over his toes and heels.

'*Consequences! Didn't I tell you?*' came a voice from high overhead. And there, on the ledge above the monkey-puzzle trees, the marred shape of Ravello pointed at Peter a steel hook in place of a hand. '*What did I tell you, cock-a-doodle? Every action has its consequences!*'

The red mire swallowed Peter to his ankles. He spread his arms wide to keep his balance. A Roarer pushed John, too, on to the red carpet of mud and elbowed Wendy after him.

Consequences

There was no fear in Pan's face, only a sad bewilderment that the Roarers should feel so badly done by. 'You all swore to keep the Rule and not to grow up. Why did you grow bigger, if you didn't want to be banished?'

'We was poisoned, innit?' said the roughest one. 'Poisoned by a dirty double-dealing twister of a chief.' And he swung at Pan's head with his branch, and missed. The look of injured reproach on Peter's face would have softened the hardest heart . . . if the Roarers had had any hearts to soften.

'Peter didn't betray you!' said Wendy. '*There* is the man who betrayed you!' And she pointed up at Hook. '*He* is the one who made you grow! If it hadn't been for Hook you could have stayed young for ever, just like Peter! And been able to fly and to come and go and visit your mothers and keep your promises and go questing after treasure six days in any week!' She let out an involuntary yelp of disgust as the soupy redness reached the hem of her dress. Peter was already sunk to his waist, arms held high to keep his hands clean of mud.

'Hook?' The Roarers were confused by the name. '*Captain* Hook?' It reminded them of their days in the Wendy House, listening to stories of the villainous pirate eaten by a crocodile before they were even born. ''Snot Hook. Tha's the circus man!'

'. . . travelling man.'

'. . . ravelling man.'

Each knew the man on the mountainside, but not as Jas. Hook, only as someone they had met on their travels.

'Wendy is right. He is the one who poisoned Neverland!' shouted Peter, chest-deep now in the mire. 'Tell them, Hook! Tell them how the bottle in your breast pocket leaked poison and killed the crocodile!—poisoned the Lagoon!—let in Time, and turned my Lost Boys into Roarers!'

And Hook laughed and bowed one last time to Peter— no longer the servile bow of a valet, but the arrogant flourish of a victor acknowledging cheers.

Each of the Roarers could remember meeting the ravelling man. A few could remember the feel of the greasy wool in their hands, and answering the question— *'What do you want to be when you grow up, boy?'* None realized till now that they had met the notorious Captain James Hook.

Captain James Hook saw the Roarers drop their branches and, like a turning tide, start back towards him. They were roaring in that low crescendo of hate that gave them their name. *'Hook! Hook! Hook! Hook!'* they chanted—reaching the cliff—starting up the trees. Within minutes they would scramble up to the ledge where he stood. He raised the fingers of his left hand to his mouth . . . and blew.

Consequences

It was a startling, quacking noise, which made the Roarers falter in their climb, the quagmire falter in its eager sucking. The ferns and heather of the plain stirred in swashing eddies, and, looking down, the Roarers recoiled in shock. For twelve lions and a family of bears, three tigers and a cotillo; ponies, a puma, and a palmerion were coming at their master's call. Instinct taught the animals the safe routes through the bogs; loyalty taught them their duty: to save the Great Ravello from danger, and to slaughter his foes.

The Roarers scattered—each man for himself—dropping their loot, throwing aside the rainbow banner. Like a firework exploding, they were invisible five seconds later. Some of the beasts gave chase and others stood snuffing the air; some prowled to and fro, looking for a way up to the master who had summoned them. The bears were sidetracked by the hives in the trees.

Meanwhile, John had sunk in the mire up to his knees, Wendy to her waist, but Peter's chin was already beneath the sucking mud. The Twins snatched up one of the branches dropped by the Roarers and leaned out towards him as far as they dared. But then and there, in front of their very eyes, taking one last gasp of air, Peter sank under; nothing remained but two pale hands growing like fennel out of the smooth red moss.

And the branch did not reach!

'PETER!'

'Pass me that other branch there!' said John. 'And keep back from the edge!'

But John's branch could not reach Peter either.

'Give me one, too!' said Wendy. '. . . And hold still, John, or you'll sink faster!' The Twins threw a branch to John who passed it to Wendy and she reached out with it as far as her arms would let her.

At the touch of rough wood, the pale hands closed into fists. Then Wendy pulled, and John pulled her, and the Twins pulled John, and slowly, slowly, red feathers, coppery leaves, brown mud, and bright blue eyes came to light.

Like spring after winter.

Like the story of the Giant Turnip, they dragged Peter (and each other) to firm ground. And the band of friends saved themselves and each other from the terrible grip of the crimson quicksand.

Panting and coughing and spitting and complaining about the mud in their knickers, they lay on solid ground, looking very like the branches that lay between them, laughing up at the sky. Such a lovely sky! with shreds and dabbles of rainbow in it.

Then into their field of vision, into that sky, poked the leathery button nose of a bear. And into their mud-clogged ears came the throaty grumbling of lions discussing their next meal. And into their faces came the warm breath of twenty assorted beasts closing in for the kill.

CHAPTER TWENTY-THREE
The Red Coat

If Time truly stood still in Neverland, then nothing at all would happen. A lion's open mouth would never close in a bite. A ravening bear would stand still, like a stuffed exhibit in a museum. But Time never stood *that* still in Neverland, not even Before. Things happen all the time in Neverland, and some are wonderful and some are utterly deadly.

Two seconds more and they would be cat meat. Two minutes more and they would be bones. They were outnumbered. Just one of the bears could have outnumbered them all by itself, but there were five, prancing in dance-time—1-2-3, 1-2-3—as once they had in the ring. The lions' hot breath smelt of dead rabbit, and there were bird bones between the palmerion's pin-sharp teeth. Circus ponies, the charred stumps of plumes still sticking up from their browbands, pounded round and round, hemming the children in: there was no escape.

Wendy pretended they were nightmares and would go away at any moment.

The Twins thought of mothers and how one should come now and put a stop to the game.

John thought of a pistol he had found once under his pillow—once, long ago when he had been grown-up—and how, if he had just brought that pistol . . .

But First Twin thought of the red coat. He had brought it down from the mountain, sleeves knotted around his waist. Now he wrestled it loose and threw it into the air, and the downward slash of a bear's claws caught it and snagged it and carried it aloft as the creature tried to shake it free. The lions, excited by movement, leapt up at it, saliva splashing like rain. The red meant nothing to them, colour-blind all, but the thrashing of the coat and the flashing of its buttons in the sunlight teased and agitated them. Hind paws trampled the children on the ground as the circus beasts tussled for the red frock coat.

Red mattered to Peter, though. Peter had been looking up at the sky, and now Red mattered so much that he shouted it at the top of his lungs: '*RED! RED! RED! RED!*

DO YOU SEE? RED!'

Out of the sky fell flakes of a colour they had all seen once before. A confetti of fairies. A handful, a fistful, a crateful, a tubful, a cartload, a torrent of fairies.

As the animals looked up in surprise, and batted paws at the strange downfall of prettiness, the children squirmed away to hide in among the swamp reeds. So when the Blue fairy army fell in earnest on the red coat, it felled only the animals. Claws and teeth were useless against such an onslaught. The gaping jaws were soon crammed solid with prickly fairies; paws were soon pinned to the ground. Lion and bear, cottilo, tiger, and all were buried so deep under a drift of hooligan fairies that not a whisker or a tail or an ear was left showing.

'*Let them go!*'

Somehow, by jumping and clambering and sliding and then by falling the rest of the way, Ravello descended the cliffs at the base of Neverpeak. In a matter of moments he was at the bottom (though the monkey-puzzle trees had taken their toll) and was running towards the fray. 'Let them go! Get them off, Pan! Help my beasts!'

Like a swarm of locusts, the fairies formed a shimmering, shifting, crackling net over the captive animals. These were fairies of the Blue Faction and believed they had just won a great victory over the forces of Redness. They thought it with one mind—as the ants in an anthill think like a single brain.

And their single-mindedness told them not to shift until the life was crushed out of the red-loving opposition.

Ravello ran the whole way, brandishing the oar from among his Treasure. The corkscrew-dogwoods plucked at him as he passed, as if to say, *Too late, too late*. 'Let them go, you vermin! They cannot breathe! They cannot move!' And he began shovelling up fairies with the blue-green rowing blade, and pitching their tiny bodies into the air. A parent with children buried under rubble would not have dug with more frenzy. It was useless: the fairies were no sooner in the air than they dived back down into the scrum. 'Help me, Pan! Don't just stand there! Can't you hear them crying? They're afraid! They're suffocating! They cannot move!' And the breath wheezed in his own throat, as though he was back inside the crocodile and suffocating himself. 'Help me free them, Pan! Lend a hand, you idle whelp!'

'And have them *eat* us? Are you mad?' Peter took up his favourite stance, feet apart, hands on hips, defiantly young.

'They are beasts! I did not set them on you! They follow their instincts! There is no malice in them. Not like these . . . these . . . *insects*! Hush, cub-bages, I am coming! Calmly, cat-kins, Ravello is here. What are you waiting for, Pan?'

Peter tilted his head on one side and gave a twinkling smile. 'What's the little word that gets things done?' he enquired gleefully.

Ravello went rigid. He straightened up. 'To think I suffered you to wear my school tie round that worthless little throat. When I was your valet, I should have tied it tighter for you—tighter by *far!*'

Peter raised one hand, and the fingers beckoned for Hook to give him the right answer. 'What's the little word?'

Ravello stared at him. 'I see now why the swamp spat you out,' he said.

But Peter spoke the little sing-song chant again, determined to make Hook say 'please' for the first time in his reprehensible life. 'What's the little . . .'

'*PITY!*' roared Ravello, and the horizons of Neverland twanged like bowstrings, and North and South swapped ends.

Then Wendy ran and grabbed up the crumpled rainbow banner from where the Roarers had dropped it. She shook the rumples out with a crack that made the boys jump, and laid it on top of the fairy mound like a tablecloth. 'Here! Here's a new banner for you, fairies! The prettiest in Neverland! Now go away and pick on someone your own size!'

Dazzled and distracted by something so shiny, the fairies allowed themselves to fall skywards, taking the banner with them, dividing up its rainbow colours between them—*I'll have this one.' 'I want that one!*—as they drifted away to make war on someone their own size instead of fifty times bigger.

'Peter . . . how did you know they were the Blue Army?' asked John in a whisper.

'Lucky guess!' Peter was jubilant.

The animals from Ravello's circus looked flatter than paper cut-outs. They lay along the ground glassy-eyed, winded, their legs at all angles, tails kinked, whiskers nibbled short by the thuggish fairies. Ravello went down on his knees, stroking flanks, untucking fragile limbs, crooning encouragement to them. He paused only to glower at Peter with eyes the colour of burning peat. '*Now* I will fight you, Pan,' he said. '*Now* I will fight you.'

'I am ready, Hook.'

One by one the animals got shakily to their feet, whimpering and whining, here and there raising a paw to touch Ravello's cuff, remembering some circus trick that had brought them a treat in the past. Then they tottered away to lick their wounds, melding with the yellow of the spilled hives, with the brown of the grassless earth. The ferns and heathers of the great plain swashed with eddies of movement, and they were gone. Not one animal remained in the shadow of Neverpeak.

Then Ravello advanced on Peter, unearthing his hook from the tangle of his right sleeve. He did not seem to see the other children, but came at Peter like a privateer closing on a treasure ship. 'Have at thee, boy!' He was Roarer through and through.

'I have no sword, pirate.'

'Then this time I have the advantage. Last time we

fought, you had the power of flight. Not quite within the spirit of the Game, I always thought. Have at thee, I say!'

If you think he slipped and the swamp swallowed him, you are quite wrong.

If you think that the fairies returned—or that John found he had brought that pistol after all—or that Slightly and Curly came back—or that Tootles summoned the police, then you still do not understand how deadly a place Neverland can be.

'*Consequences!*' said Hook, slashing at Peter's head. 'All acts have consequences, you see!'

Peter ducked and wove, leapt away, dodged behind the cork trees; but Ravello came after him brandishing a dagger in his left hand, and swinging with his right. Jay feathers flew like gouts of blood, as the hook slashed Peter's tunic. Peter's bare soles recoiled from sharp stones underfoot: he scrabbled up the stones and threw them at Ravello, but they lifted only puffs of dust from the shaggy fleece and, just once, the sound of an egg breaking. Peter clicked his tongue and made the sound of a clock ticking, but the thought of crocodiles no longer frightened Hook— it only enraged him. A crooked branch snagged Peter's collar and held him, like fruit ripe for the picking. Hook stopped for a moment to savour the sight of his enemy vainly struggling, powerless to save himself. Then he considered in what soft part of Peter's body to sink the killing blow.

Oh.

Did I say there were no animals left in the shadow of Neverpeak? No circus animals, I meant. There was one that had come there to cock its leg against a dogwood tree. Like everything in Neverland, this animal was a little . . . changed. As a consequence of tangling in Ravello's fleece, little Puppy had aged since falling off the mountain. And when a Newfoundland puppy ages, there is quite an alteration.

Out it came now: a hound half as high as a horse, bouncy as ever but thirty times as big. Puppy was as big now as its great-grandmother, Nana the Nursery-Nurse-Hound, and its devotion was every bit as huge. It went to Peter's rescue with bark and bite and snarl and claws, and it did not let go—got snaggled and *couldn't* let go—pulled and struggled and scrabbled and bit, until Hook lay like a hank of dead mermaid's hair on the shore of a poisoned Lagoon.

John gathered up the Treasure scattered between the red swamp and the trees: cups and trophies and caps. He looked around for something to carry it all in, and found the red coat lying ripped and discarded on the ground.

'Leave it,' said Pan, generous in victory. 'It is not my kind of treasure. I do not need it.' And that was true, because the boy in the leafy tunic and bare feet and caking of mud showed no likeness at all to Captain James Hook. 'Leave it all.'

Nurse Tootles might have liked to practise bandaging, or making a sling, but she did not have the courage to go anywhere near the unravelled man on the ground. So it was Wendy who finally went and crouched down beside Ravello. She had sewn potholders. She had sewn traycloths and aprons. She had once even sewn a boy's shadow back on when it came adrift. But her powers of needlework did not stretch to this particular piece of mending.

'Are you dying, Mr Ravello?' she asked.

'I fear, lady, that I am . . . *undone*, yes. I thank you for rescuing my animals.'

'It was a little bit our fault they got squashed.' She tucked the blue-green oar under his arm, like a hot-water bottle, and stacked the trophies and cups in a shining silver pyramid, where he could see them as he died. 'Some of these got rather bent, I'm afraid.'

'Their worth is not in their condition, madam.' His eyes rested on them with ineffable joy. 'You know—I may return them if ever I am invited back to address the School on Speech Day.'

'That would be a very interesting Speech Day, Mr Ravello.'

'Hook! My name is Hook, madam. Captain James Hook.'

Wendy reminded him of Doctor Curly's advice: 'Sleep is a great healer, you know? You should sleep.'

For a second Hook's eyes flashed bitter resentment. 'Madam, I have not slept for twenty years. Not since the crocodile!'

'I expect that's because you haven't had anyone to kiss you goodnight—not since the crocodile, anyway.'

The great straggling tangle that was James Hook writhed like an old fishing net caught in a rising tide. His voice was weak but there was no mistaking the strength of his feelings. 'Madam, I have *never* had anyone kiss me goodnight! Mine was not that breed of mother. In any case, it would be vulgar and namby-pamby and sentimental and . . . and not quite *manly*.'

Wendy nodded and patted his hand. 'But worth a try?'

'But worth a try,' conceded Captain Hook.

So even though he was the blood-thirstiest pirate on all the seven seas and hated her friend Peter Pan more than Death itself, Wendy bent and kissed Hook on the cheek, then covered him over with the rags of the red frock coat. 'Goodnight, James,' she said, in her most motherly voice. 'Sweet dreams.' Then she left him alone, knowing that

Death would be along shortly to cradle him in gentle and forgiving arms.

Peter saw it and he was furious—really quite astonishingly furious, considering he was no longer wearing the red frock coat. His cheeks flushed and he called Wendy a traitor. 'Hook is the Enemy! If you are nice to my enemies, you must be my enemy, too!' And he went for his sword.

He had no sword, of course; he looked at the others, but they had no swords either, because the Roarers had taken them all. Besides, no one wanted to lend Peter a sword for the killing of Wendy. Unfortunately, Peter was not deterred. With every passing hour the power of Imagination was returning to him. So he simply unsheathed an imaginary sword and used that—'*Oh, Peter, no!*'—to cut a door in the air.

'A french window for me, if you please!' said Wendy defiantly, and Peter, taken aback, made the door into a pair of french windows instead.

'Wendy Darling, I banish you to Nowhereland for giving succour to the enemy! Go now!'

'The door jambs are not straight,' said Wendy and folded her arms.

John sprang forward and opened the doors, not because he wanted his sister to be banished, but because he had been nicely brought up and knew to open a door for a lady. There was a look of stricken misery on the Twins' faces. Wendy politely thanked her brother and stepped through the french windows, head held high.

Peter Pan had been expecting her to beg forgiveness and speak the-little-word-that-gets-things-undone. But now she was outside, in Nowhereland, and had not said Sorry at all! He fumbled sheathing his imaginary sword, and dropped it on his foot. And because he could not think what else to do, he shut the french windows and shot the bolts top and bottom. Tootles burst into tears.

Wendy did not look very punished. She did not even look very banished, standing there on the far side of the door with her arms crossed. 'Stand away, please,' she said sharply, and the boys stepped smartly backwards—even Peter Pan. Then Wendy bent down, picked up an imaginary boulder and hurled it through the imaginary french windows. There was the most tremendous smash of breaking glass. 'Bosh and tosh!' she said, stepping through the wreckage of glazing bars and locks and bolts, being careful not to tear her pirate-flag dress on the jagged glass. 'Sometimes, Peter, you are *such* a ninny!'

John had never heard his sister say either 'bosh' or 'tosh', and certainly not both at once. His mouth dropped open and he brushed some imaginary glass out of her hair. As Wendy led the way briskly along the narrow pathway and out of the shadow of Neverpeak, the others fell into step behind her.

'Should you have done that, sis?' whispered First Twin. He had to trot just to keep up.

'It is quite all right,' said Wendy. 'I bent my knees and kept my back straight. I know to be very careful lifting boulders.'

And beyond that no more was said.

By the next day, Peter Pan had forgotten all about the quarrel. He was always good at forgetting things he did not want to remember.

CHAPTER TWENTY-FOUR
Back Together

Having neither the power of flight nor a ship to sail, the Company of Pan knew they had to walk clear across the island to reach the Neverwood again. Without the power of flight or the gift of fairy dust or the company of half the Company, it seemed a very long way indeed. Out there lurked Roarers and injured beasts, hostile fairies and homeless harpy birds, thirsty deserts and junior pirates, witches, dragons, swamps and unpredictable puddles.

They were toiling up a particularly wearisome hill, expecting to find below them the waterless wastes of the Thirsty Desert, when the sky ahead turned ochre yellow with flying dust. Sandstorm, they thought. Then they topped the rise, and a sight met their eyes that none would ever forget. There, streaming towards them across the flat skillet of the sear desert sands, came all the bison and appaloosas and travois and squaws and dogs and braves and thunderbirds and drums and papooses and war bonnets and peace-pipes and braids and coup sticks and moccasins and bows and arrows that went to make up the Tribes of the Eight Nations.

The smoke signals Peter had sent from the top of Neverpeak had not been smudged out completely. Now Tribes from north, south, east, west and the other place came thundering over the Thirsty Desert as fast as their appaloosas and bison would carry them. At the sight of Peter and his fellow Explorers, they began to bang on their shields and drums and papooses and so forth in a triumphant chorus of greeting.

The Tribes threw a potlatch for the League: a party that consisted of eating and drinking and giving away most of their belongings. They gave a lot of these to Peter and Wendy and Tootles and the Twins and John (who was thrilled to the core). But sadly, because they had nothing of their own to give, the children had to give away the gifts they had just been given.

At the feast that followed, a lovely Princess came and smeared their faces with warpaint and told them that now they were honorary members of the Eight Nations.

'Hello, Tiger Lily,' said Peter. But the Princess looked at him strangely and said she was Princess Agapanthus, actually. 'Ah. I could never remember names,' Peter said. 'Or faces.'

'Twins? Whatever is the matter?' asked Tootles. 'Just because you had to give away those bowie knives . . .'

But the Twins were not crying because of the bowie knives. They had just remembered riding on an omnibus to Putney and falling asleep and waking to find themselves wearing warpaint. 'Will we ever see Putney again, Wendy?' they asked.

Wendy put on her most businesslike face. 'We shall just have to wait for the fairies to stop quarrelling and for our shadows to grow back. Look: yours are starting to come already.' The Twins brightened—then, of course, their shadows stopped growing again, which rather defeated Wendy's efforts.

They travelled on in a cloud of dust, with an escort of Eight Nations (not to mention the bison)—through the Elephants' Graveyard, over Parcel Pass and the primaeval ruins of Never City and the Groves of Academe. If there were Roarers or lions lying in ambush, the bison and travoises flattened them, because suddenly the horizon was plush with the trees of Neverwood, and the Tribes were saying goodbye and moving off in eight different directions—to tepees, hogans, kivas or longhouses, roundhouses, bivouacs or stockades; some to sleep under the stars.

'Where will *we* sleep tonight?' asked Tootles.

The Nevertree still lay where it had fallen in the storm, like a giant crossing-out. What a long way they had come to reach home, half forgetting that home was not where they had left it. Its leaves had all burned off in the fire.

'Tomorrow we can all start to build Fort Pan,' said Peter, but it did not quite answer where they were going to sleep.

In the end, it was Puppy who served as a bed. It lay down on its side, and the Explorers curled up between front and back legs, in among the fur. Puppy was no great shakes as a nursemaid—licked them over a bit before bedtime, but forgot tooth brushing or prayers. Secretly, it was missing Slightly and Curly and that interesting chewy man who had smelt of eggs and cough drops and fear. While the Company of Pan looked up at the stars, Wendy told them all a fairy story about a little white bird in Kensington Gardens. A warm breeze blew through the Neverwood.

All of a sudden, without a word of warning and with an upheaval that rolled everyone on top of everyone else, Puppy stood up. It lolloped off into the trees and did not stop till it had searched out Peter's old underground den. Then it began to dig.

Now Puppy, when it was a puppy, had wanted nothing but to get out of Peter Pan's underground den as quickly as possible after falling in. But now that it stood four feet tall at the shoulder it was more ambitious. It could hear and smell the Something underground, and was determined to get in. By the time the Explorers arrived on the scene, Puppy had dug a hole big enough to bury a treasure chest.

John called: 'Careful, Puppy! You will go through the . . .'

  'R

     o

       o

         f !'said Puppy (or something like it) and arrived abruptly in the den where Peter had once lived with his Lost Boys. Now the Something was bound to emerge, be it badger, slaggoth, or giant truffle, and the weary travellers stood transfixed, awaiting the awful sight.

Several things in fact emerged from the hole in the den roof, some quicker than others:

—candlelight

—barking

—music (broken off short)

—yelps of fright

—the noise of breaking furniture

—Puppy's panting

—no candlelight

—that distinctive sound people make when licked on the neck in the dark

—then a white flag of surrender. (Well, actually it was pink and tied to a walking stick, but it was the only handkerchief available and it is hard to tell pink from white in the dark.)

—then Slightly-more,

—and Dr Curly MD, MRCS,

—and Smee, erstwhile First Mate to Hook, blood-thirstiest pirate ever to sail the seven seas.

'Well done, Curly! Well done, Slightly! Did you take him prisoner? Did you? Did you fight him with your bare hands?' said John, breaking Smee's pink flag across his knee.

'Certainly not,' said Slightly, relighting the candles. 'He made us a nice cup of tea. Apparently Mr Smee has been living here for years. He has made the place very cosy.'

'What is it now, then, a bandits' hideout?' asked John, rubbing his knee.

'More of a retirement home, I think,' said Dr Curly.

Nobody thought twice about talking to Slightly or Curly, despite them being big. (That must have had something to do with the smashing of the french windows.) As for Smee, he busied round righting tables and taping enough chairs back together for everyone to sit down.

'I thought Hook sent you off to do your bit in the Big War?' said Tootles to him.

'Me and the rest of us, yes he did. The others got . . . lost. Afterwards I was on me own. So I travelled 'bout giving talks 'bout life aboard the *Jolly Roger*, and how Smee was the only man James Hook ever feared.'

'I think I saw a poster,' said Curly.

'Is that true, Mr Smee? That James Hook was afraid of you?'

'Faith no, boy! What's the truth got to do with show business? But a man has to live. In the end, I got too afeared—that Hook would hear of it and hunt me down and cut out me lying tongue, or some such. Soft-headed, I know, but I used to dream him come squirming out of that old crocodile to haunt me, hook glinting and me name all twisted up on his lips: *Smeeee!*' (The Explorers glanced at one another, but no one broke the bad news to Smee that his dreams were not far wide of the mark.) 'I got the heeby-jeebies and chucked the lecture circuit and took up selling household cleaning products door-to-door. Mops. Sponges. Scouring pads, that manner of thing.' (The underground den certainly did look very clean and tidy and was very well stocked with sponges, scouring pads, and mops and that manner of thing.) '. . . But I missed this place. Neverland, I mean.' He looked about him as though the small earth-walled burrow where he lived contained Neverland entire. 'So I nicked a pram and sailed back here.'

'But you aren't a child!' said John, impressed.

'Nah. But there was a shortage of pirates, thanks to you lot, so I got permission. I'd kill for chocolate money: reckon that makes me near enough a Lost Boy.'

'But you don't work as a pirate any more?'

'Nah. Gave it a try, but me heart wasn't in it, somehow. Not without a captain. Or a ship. Starkey calls round sometimes for rum and scones. We spin a yarn or two. Generally there's not much I miss—though I'm rare fond of talcum powder, and that can't be had in Neverland. Not for real money. Well, not even for chocolate money, which is 'stonishing!'

'There was some aboard the *Jolly Roger*,' said Wendy.

'That was gunpowder, lassie. It's not the same. Been a quiet sort of a life, all in all, since I came here. Till tonight, that is. What's that horrible dog of yours doing now? I don't crochet table-mats for dogs to do that with them.' They rescued the crochet work from Puppy who had been unravelling it, reminded of the chewy man who smelt of fear. 'Mr Curly and Mr Slightly here were just telling me some of their excitements on the way here. Go on, won't you, gentlemen?'

And so despite the interruption of the roof falling in and

the sudden arrival of Peter Pan and Co., Curly and Slightly took up their story again.

'We were walking back from Neverpeak, towards the Reef, thinking to build a raft or signal a passing ship, I don't know. We heard running feet behind us, and shouting. At first I thought we were being chased, but they went streaking by like things possessed—Roarers!—yelling that there were lions after them—and bears! Naturally we started running too, but those boys must have been chased oftener than us, because we were left trailing. They tore on like madmen, not looking where they were going, right, Slightly?'

'We shouted a warning when we saw where they were heading. But they were too busy running—straight into the Maze of Witches!'

'We never saw the lions, did we, Slightly?'

'No, but we saw the Witches!'

'They were on the Roarers in a twinkling. It was horrible!'

'Those women lifted grown lads clean off the ground—held them so tight they stopped struggling inside the minute! We hid, didn't we, Slightly?'

'We should have tried to rescue them. But we hid. I would have played my clarinet, but I hadn't the breath for it.'

'So we hid.'

'We did.'

Tootles could not wait: 'And did the Witches EAT the Roarers?'

The two were slow to answer. They were picturing once again the horrific round-up in the Maze of Witches, as one by one the Roarers were captured. They could not forget the women's shrill shrieks of triumph, their plunging faces aimed at throat or nose or ears (difficult to tell from a distance) and the way each prisoner gradually stopped struggling and went limp within the clutches of his captor. Slightly and Curly sank their heads in their hands and rocked with sorrow that they had not done more to help.

Smee, meanwhile, ate a muffin. 'Poor souls,' he said through a cheerful mouthful of crumbs. 'Now I suppose they will have to go through it all—the baths, the haircuts, the kisses—the night-night songs from people as couldn't carry a tune if you gave 'em a bucket. All those satchels and chest rubs and woollen swimming drawers and great-aunts. Tapioca! But I don't know why you style them "witches". Those females ain't witches.' He rummaged in a pencil box for a tube of liquorice, which he cleaned with a pipe cleaner before sucking on it like a pipe. Only then did he notice that the others were staring at him. 'What?'

'But it's called the Maze of Witches. Of course they are witches!' said Tootles.

Smee snorted scornfully. 'Who told you that?'

'Captain H—'

'—Mr Ravello the circus master told us!' said John drowning out Tootles. And he recounted the sad story of nursery maids sacked, turned out-of-doors, mad with hatred and seeking revenge on the children of Neverland. 'Maze of Witches,' he called it. Perhaps you're thinking of some other place.'

Smee bit the end off his liquorice pipe and chewed it till his spit ran black. 'Stripy rocks all carved out by water? Close by Grief Reef? Your Mr Ravello don't know his witches from his whats. Don't know his aunts from his bilboes. That there's the Maze of Regrets! Nursery maids? Codswallop! No hired servant would set sail over stormy seas in an open perambulator—not out of hate, not out of anything! Nah! Those ladies there are the Heartbroken! There's none other would make a voyage like that. They do what they have to. Instinct, see. Can't help theirselves. They'd do *anything*, Mothers would.'

CHAPTER TWENTY-FIVE
The Heartbroken

They stood once more on high ground, the sea a distant flicker and the grass balding away to rock beneath their feet. The Maze of Regrets, with its striped strata and crests as sharp as elbows, lay directly ahead. It leaked the sound of sorrow and a strange mixture of old perfumes.

'This is dangerous,' said Peter Pan.

Wendy laid a hand on his sleeve, but he shook it off, saying, 'I must not be touched.'

'But Slightly and Curly have to go home,' said Wendy for the fiftieth time. 'They are too big to live at Fort Pan, and they are just not the stuff of Roarers—or pirates—or redskins.'

And here was their Way Out, their Emergency Exit from Neverland: the Maze. In this place, the mothers of Lost Boys passed their years searching for the babies they had once lost. The carelessness of nursery maids could not be blamed in every case. (Lots of parents cannot afford nursery maids.) Even with parents in charge, babies go missing—fall out of prams, run away with the bath water, or get put out instead of the cat. Mistakes happen in the best regulated households.

When they do, the result is always the same. Somewhere, a mother packs herself a bag, pushes the empty pram to the local docks—Grimsby or Marseilles or Valparaiso—and sets sail. Keeping the red buoys to her prow and the green buoys to her stern, she goes in search of her lost b~~uo~~y . . . boy, in a place worn smooth by millions of tears. Without the magic to advance further into Neverland, she ends up here, in the Maze of Regrets, living from day to day on egg-and-cress sandwiches and the hope that her little boy will one day come whistling round the next corner in the Maze.

The Roarers, when they spilled unwittingly into the Maze, had been seized on like bargains in a sale. Wild-haired women with wilder eyes had grabbed them and searched their faces for family features, their bodies for birthmarks. Youths who had tried never even to brush against one another had been stroked and kissed and hugged—washed with tears and wiped clean with lace handkerchiefs. What Slightly and Curly had witnessed was not a massacre. It was a reunion!

Among the Roarers, a dozen mothers had found what they were looking for, and had left Neverland with their sulking, hulking sons. Even as they climbed back into their sea-going perambulators at Grief Reef, the mothers had started to polish up manners and brush down clothes.

You see, any mother who searches out her Lost Boy can find her way home unerringly. The voyage might be long and dangerous, and tankers and luxury liners sometimes run them down in the sea lanes, but their homing instinct is as strong as that of Canada geese or messenger pigeons. Home signals to them like a flashing beacon on a distant clifftop. They are almost bound to get there.

Now it was the turn of Slightly and Curly to enter the Maze, and no terror that had faced them on their quest to Neverpeak compared with the quaking fright they felt now. Being grown-ups—Slightly a youth of eighteen, Curly a fully-fledged doctor—they could not let their fright show, of course, but smoothed their hair and straightened their collars and polished their shoes against the backs of their trouser-legs. (That was hard for Slightly since he was barefoot and had no trousers. But at least his evening shirt fitted; unlike the pullover that Smee had knitted for Curly during the journey from the Neverwood.)

'But we already *have* a mother!' Slightly protested yet again. 'Mrs Darling adopted us!'

'Yes, dear, but even *before* Mother adopted you, you and all the Lost Boys had mothers of your own—somewhere.'

'Mine won't be here,' said Curly dismally. 'She won't have come looking—not all this way.'

'She will,' said Wendy, and stood on tiptoe to kiss him on the jaw.

'And even if she don't,' said Tootles off-handedly, 'one of those women will probably think you're hers and take you home.'

'Well then,' said Curly.

'This is it, then,' said Slightly.

'Till London,' said John.

'Till London,' said Curly.

'Safe journey,' said Wendy. 'Give our love to Nibs.'

'Don't drown,' said Tootles, and shed a tear or two.

Peter turned his back and would not shake hands. He could not understand why anyone wanted to leave Neverland. He had offered to try and *pretend* Slightly and Curly back to a tolerable size but they had chosen to come here instead. Now Peter could not wait to get back to the Neverwood. Games were calling. Quests were piling up. There was a fort to be built. 'Go on, then,' he said. 'Go, if you are going.'

The Heartbroken

Curly and Slightly-more would also have liked to help build Fort Pan. But the thought of homes and wives and work and Nibs and London buses was working its magic on both young men. They squared their shoulders and walked down to the Maze. Curly turned back only once: 'I was so young when I got Lost. How will Mummy know me?' he said, and for a moment he looked a littler boy than anyone there.

'She will,' said Wendy. 'She just will.'

Slightly put his clarinet to his lips and began to play. Curly led the way. Their anxious friends drifted downhill behind them, to watch what became of them.

Women harassed by years of woe and worry lifted their heads at the sound of music. They blinked in confusion at the sight of a youth and a grown man, for they had thought this a place of children, and children were what filled their every thought. They did not fall on Curly, for none could imagine . . . none had been expecting . . . anyone like this. He shook hands. The women tucked away stray wisps of hair; some even bobbed a curtsy. Soothed by the music and taken by surprise, they allowed Curly to speak, and the watching children could see him explaining, describing, pointing back the way he had come.

Then he must have mentioned his own name, for through the growing throng of mothers came a woman, lunging like a horse in deep water, stretching and ducking to catch a glimpse, pushing her way through. Plaits that for thirty years had stayed neatly coiled came flying loose and she collided with Curly head-on. The League of Pan shut their eyes . . . and when they opened them again, Curly was helping his mother to refasten her hair.

Slightly looked up from a particularly difficult key change on the clarinet to find a thin woman with long thin fingers and a thin, artistic face staring at him. 'You didn't take this, my darling,' she said. 'When you went missing.' And she produced a baby's rattle with bells at either end.

Then and there, Slightly's tunes—the ones in his head, the ones in his clarinet, and the ones in his heart—all came back to doh.

That was when the Twins strayed a little too close to the Maze and heard someone calling: '*Marmaduke? Binky?*'

Now this may come as a shock to you if you thought that the two brothers really were named First Twin and Second Twin at birth. They weren't. True, they were lost at such an early age that their names were no more than a memory forgotten. But when their mother—hands still clarty with pastry, hair still dusty with flour—came running and staring and blinking and crying and laughing and breaking into a run—'*Marmaduke? Binky?*'—they remembered well enough.

Marmaduke and Binky. Ah well. Everyone makes mistakes. Luckily, the Twins took to the names as no one else could, and thought themselves the luckiest boys in the world. For now they had *two* mothers! Mrs Darling would always be the real one, because she had taken them in when they were Lost Boys, and had raised them and let them lick the mixing bowl and shampoo the dog and wear warpaint in bed and ride upstairs on buses . . . But here was a NEW mother from longer ago—the one who had given them the best two names in the world.

Wendy turned to Tootles. 'You could go home this way, too, you know, Princess?'

Tootles shook her head very decidedly. 'I'm not going ever!' she said. 'I'm going to stay here for always and play weddings with Peter!'

A fox in a chicken coop could not have caused more of a stir. Wendy looked at Peter, and Peter looked at Wendy, and there was real panic in his eyes.

'Tootles! You know very well you have a family waiting for you back in Grimswater,' said John. But sadly Tootles had forgotten all about Grimswater or The Gentlemen's Club or being a judge in the High Courts.

'I'll be Tootles Pan, and Peter can pick flowers for me and lift up his feet when I am sweeping, and I'll say to the little ones, "Just you wait till your father comes home!"'

For some reason—I couldn't say why—Wendy chose that exact moment to run into the Maze calling, *'Tootles! There's a Tootles here! Has anyone lost a Tootles?'*

A man with a face the colour of morocco leather in a curly lawyer's wig and with a huge book under one arm stepped out from behind a rock. He wagged a finger at her sternly. 'Do not be absurd, young lady!' he said, looking Wendy up and down. 'Are you trying to pass yourself off as my boy Tootles? Absurd! Poppycock!' But just as he was opening his book to look up which law Wendy had broken, he caught sight of Princess Tootles, tying the ribbons of her satin ballet shoes and practising her plié. 'Aha! There you are, son,' he said gruffly, without a moment's doubt. 'And about time, too!' Then, in an outburst of uncontrollable delight, he took off his judge's wig, threw it high in the air and danced a little jig on the spot.

'Fathers, too,' murmured Smee. 'Who'd've thought it.'

Sitting astride his father's shoulders and wearing his father's wig, Tootles rode off without a backward glance. Wendy looked at Peter, and Peter looked at Wendy, and there was a big 'THANK YOU' written in his eyes.

'Can we go, too, sis?' asked John, infected by all the happiness. It was an odd infection—it made the pouches under his chin ache, like mumps. He began to look this way and that in search of a mother who would choose him.

Wendy's heart too, was cram-full with the longing to get home and see her own daughter Jane. But she knew this was not *her* Emergency Exit, not *her* Way Out of Neverland. 'There is no one here for us, John. We were never Lost, remember? We flew to Neverland of our own choosing—and home again before Mother could set sail to come looking.' But she could see John still looking about, still wondering: how life would have been with another mother; a different mother; that one there with the blonde hair or that one there with the red. 'We shall just stay here, John, until our shadows grow back . . . and the fairies stop being silly and we can ask them for fairy dust . . . and Fort Pan is built.'

'Good,' said Peter decidedly. 'I don't mind *you*. You play proper games.'

'Nothing to stop you a-coming with me!' said Smee, rolling into the conversation on his sailor's bandy legs. 'I'm in need of a crew for the voyage home! Reckon I'll pay a visit to the old country, now I've got me a mother aboard for luck.' Small as he was, Smee had managed to find someone even smaller to clutch the crook of his arm: a tiny old lady with snow-white hair and an angelic smile.

Wendy clapped her hands with joy. 'Oh, how wonderful! This is *your* mother, Smee?'

Smee spoke from behind his hand. 'Nah. I nicked her. But her eyes aren't up to much, so she'll never notice. And she seems glad to have me. So, who else is coming, eh? Look lively! All aboard the good ship *Dirty Duck*, bound for the Serpentine by way of Kirriemuir!'

*　　*　　*

They lashed together all the prams languishing on the rocks of Grief Reef, making a huge raft. Like eggs into an egg-tray, everyone heading home squeezed themselves into the hollow compartments. Even Puppy. They all fitted.

Finding somewhere for all the happiness was the only problem.

Wendy was the last left on shore. '*Come with us, Peter!*' she cried suddenly, seizing him by the hand. 'Oh, *do* come with us! I know where there are fairies to be found! And when your shadow grows back you can fly back here and . . .'

But Peter snatched his hand away. 'I don't go about with grown people,' he said, turning his back on the good ship *Dirty Duck*.

Wendy took the other hand and led him aside. 'I have a whisper for you,' she said.

'Is that like a thimble?'

It was, in a way. It made Peter's hair bristle and his neck tickle and he wanted—and didn't want—to snatch his head away as Wendy whispered in his ear. 'I've been thinking,' she said.

'You don't want to play *Weddings*?' squeaked Peter in open panic.

Wendy pulled a face. 'Peter, just suppose *your* mother . . .'

Peter's face shut like curtains at a window. 'No.'

The Heartbroken

'Oh, but, Peter! Suppose she is just like all these: still hoping to see you again one day! Maybe she even . . .'

But Peter's delicate mouth set in a hard line and he put his fingers in his ears. Once upon a time he had flown home only to find the window of his bedroom shut and barred, another boy asleep in his bed. He refused to hear anything good about mothers.

The prams, freed from the rocks, felt the far distant pull of Lodestone Rock and the *Dirty Duck* began moving out to sea. John and Curly and Slightly and Smee all shouted for Wendy to '*Come—come aboard quickly! Don't get left behind!*'

For a moment, she did not think she could leave him— her little friend Peter, as wild and fragile and beautiful as an autumn leaf blown by the wind. She did not think she could bear to miss all the games that were calling, all the quests that were piling up. She realized she did not even know where Fort Pan would be built—up in the treetops or jutting out from the precipitous cliffs or standing on stilts in the Lagoon.

But at heart the girl Wendy was a grown-up (just as all grown-ups are, at heart, children). Love of her family was dragging on her, like the far distant pull of Lodestone Rock. Just when it seemed that the space between raft and rocks was too wide even for a circus acrobat to leap, Wendy Darling sprang off the Grief Reef and landed beside her brother, aboard the good ship *Dirty Duck*.

At Smee's command, all the pram hoods were raised to catch the wind, and the raft rode the slopping swell out towards the bar. Stricken by yet one more thought, Wendy jumped to her feet, making the raft pitch and the passengers yelp. She called out to the boy on the shore:

'*I think your mother only shut the window to keep out the FOG!*'

She saw Peter lift his hands to cover his ears, but too late. His fingers curled into fists, as if he had caught her words out of the air—caught and heard them, like it or not. Wendy waved, and went on waving, until the dazzle off the water filled her eyes with dark.

Peter watched the raft all the way out to the bar— watched it until the dazzle off the water made it disappear. As he turned, with a skip and a jump, to set off on the long walk back to Neverwood, he was surprised to find a little frill of fresh-grown shadow riffling around his feet. No time to wonder what sadness had made it grow back. Games were calling. Quests were piling up.

Meanwhile, not very far away, an old enemy lay along the ground. He lay so still that you would have thought him dead.

But despite his injuries, Ravello had not died. For the first time in twenty years, with his second-best coat for a blanket over him and with Wendy's kiss on his cheek,

Ravello slept—a sleep deeper than the Lagoon. Sleep is a great healer, people are always saying so.

He dreamed of striped rocks with crests as sharp as elbows, grooved into gullies by a million tears. On the top of one such crest stood a woman, ragged striped skirts drawn up at the back, a long and swanlike neck. Beautiful once, she looked now like some statue in a public park worn by wind and weather. And her face was so sad, so very sad, eyes roaming to and fro, searching for something or someone. Voice brittle as lead crystal, she called over and over again: '*James! James? Where are you, James?*'

Ravello slept. Sleep is a great healer; people don't lie when they say it. Ravello slept. And his greasy fleece, shredded by dog and doctor and thorn-trees . . . *knitted up*. The ravelled, colourless wool resolved itself into flesh and cloth and hair. The shining ringlets returned. Scars smoothed. Even the colour of his eyes shifted along the spectrum, from earth-brown towards the brightness of blue.

What unravelled instead was the softness of his assumed name: Ravello—laying bare the hard, sharp shape of the old one: Hook. When after twenty days the man woke, it was James Hook who sat up and cursed the hardness of the ground; James Hook who clutched the School Cup to him in fierce rapture; James Hook who took bearings from his metal compass of a heart; James Hook who slid his arms into the sleeves of the scarlet frock coat.

It became him well.

And he became it.

Clothes can do that.

But when he glimpsed his shineless crocodile boots, the Past came back: a remembered nightmare. 'Have at you, cock-a-doodle!' The words emerged like heat from an opening furnace. 'Revenge will be sweet when we two next meet. *Have at you, Peter Pan!*'

AFTERWORD

You are quite right. There was a lot of explaining to do when they got home. Imagine their mother's surprise when the Twins took her by each hand, and trotted her home to Chertsey. Imagine her astonishment, when they took out front door keys and let themselves in, calling, 'Hello, Daddy's back!' Imagine what she said as she watched them swap clothes with their little ones and grow back—*gracious goodness!*—into full-size men.

Their children had a word or two to say about it as well.

'You took my school uniform! I got in awful trouble!'

'Shoulda taken my green pyjamies, not my red ones! My red ones are my flavourites!'

'There's mud on my ballet shoes!' (That was at Tootles's house.)

'That was my *best* rugby shirt!' (That was at Curly's). And 'Oh, Daddy! You grewed the puppy!'

At Nibs's house, Nibs drew his children on to his lap and said to the visitors, 'Tell us. Tell us *everything* that happened.'

You might think the Maze mothers felt cheated to see their Lost Boys grow suddenly to manhood, but no. Better by far to find a Lost Son, whatever age he is, than never to find him at all.

Slightly, who had no wife or children to go home to, stayed as he was: eighteen. He did not even tell his Neverland mother he was a baronet, in case she bought a book of etiquette and made him act like one. Just once, he slipped away to that jazz club to play the clarinet. But when the lights dimmed and spotlight shone, he found that he could not play the Blues any more, because he was just too happy. So he joined a dance band instead.

As for Wendy and John, they gathered up all the dregs of those troublesome dreams—the hats and arrows and sabres and pistols and hooks—and gave them to Smee, who opened a party shop in Kensington, selling 'Souvenirs of Neverland'. Of course no one believed there was any such place—except the children who bought the souvenirs.

And over the while, Wendy told Jane everything, naturally. A memory here, an adventure there. Jane thought they were bedtime stories she was hearing; when she told them back to her mother, she changed bits she did not like and added in things that had not happened; Wendy said nothing. It was lovely just to hear the words bouncing round the bedroom again: 'Neverland', 'Peter', and '**Dook-a-doodie!**' (which was the best Jane could doodle-do).

Perhaps what happened to Neverland wasn't Hook's fault, at all. Oh, he would *love* you to think it was. But maybe it wasn't the bottle of mischief in his breast pocket that leaked out and poisoned Neverland. Maybe flying debris from the Big War—shrapnel and bullets and such—made holes in the fabric between Neverland and this world. Dreams leaked out through the holes; grown-up mess leaked in. And that's when the summerlands were spoiled. For a few ticks, Time moved on where Time was never meant to, and summer turned to autumn, and draughts slithered in, and friends grew cold.

Whatever the cause, it didn't last.

You know how bruises fade? Black to purple, then greenish blue and last of all yellow? Well, Neverland healed up just like that. The snow melted and watered the Thirsty Desert. The springs welled up and refilled the rivers. Burnt Neverwood re-grew. Finally the yellow sun came out and lingered—sometimes for days on end, because it was enjoying itself too much to go to bed. The Lagoon shimmered with fish and sunlight and mermaids. Villains moored up.

Lost Boys and Girls found their way to Fort Pan.

Mothers came looking for them (of course).

The Tribes held potlatch parties and gave away everything they owned—even quite a lot of things they didn't—out of sheer joy. The fairies called a truce, though for a long time marauding bands of dandies went about ripping the rainbows out of waterfalls to sew into tunics. Never mind: the waterfalls healed up, too.

Hand in hand, Tinker Bell and Fireflyer quarrelled their way here, there, and everywhere in Neverland, inventing new colours, playing Chinese chequers with the stars, and nibbling the knees out of Wednesday to make it easier to spell. They set up in business, selling dreams to Roarers and pirates in exchange for belt buckles and buttons. It was a dangerous line of work—especially catching the dreams with a tripwire and a net—but the two fairies were so happy that they decided not to get killed for at least a hundred years.

As for Pan, it took an age for his shadow to grow all the way back, because he was so rarely sad. Only when he thought of Wendy and the others did a little more darkness flap out behind him—a leg, a narrow waist, a sword-arm . . . So he was confined to Neverland, unable to fly, and the Darlings saw nothing of him from one summer to the next.

Don't worry, though. His shadow is all there nowadays. He can fly as far and as high as he chooses—faster than dreams can flicker through your head—further afield even than Fotheringdene or Grimswater.

He has never broken his terrible habit of eavesdropping. So, maybe that wasn't the rustle of pages you heard while this story lasted, but Peter Pan himself, listening in. In exchange for a story of yours, he might show you his most prized possession: James Hook's map of Neverland.

In exchange for a smile, he may show you Neverland itself.